Suspected

By George Dilnot

Originally published in 1920

Suspected

© 2016 Resurrected Press
www.ResurrectedPress.com

Published by Resurrected Press

This classic book was handcrafted by Resurrected Press. Resurrected Press is dedicated to bringing high quality classic books back to the readers who enjoy them. These are not scanned versions of the originals, but, rather, quality checked and edited books meant to be enjoyed!

Please visit ResurrectedPress.com to view our entire catalogue!

For updates on future releases, LIKE us on Facebook: http://www.Facebook.com/ResurrectedPress

ISBN 13: 978-1-943403-33-2

Printed in the United States of America

MYSTERIES BY LEONARD GRIBBLE

Available now, or coming Soon!
Like us on Facebook to see our latest books!
http://www.facebook.com/ResurrectedPress

Is this Revenge (1931) aka The Serpentine Murder
The Stolen Home Secretary (1932) aka The Stolen
Statesman
The Yellow Bungalow (1933)
The Death Chime (1934)
The Riddle of the Ravens (1934)
Mystery at Tudor Arches (1935)
The Case of the Malverne Diamonds (1936)
Riley of the Special Branch (1936)
Who Killed Oliver Cromwell? (1937)
The Case Book of Anthony Slade (1937)
Tragedy in E Flat (1938)
The Arsenal Stadium Mystery (1939)
Atomic Murder (1947)
Hangman's Moon (1950)
They Kidnapped Stanley Matthews (1950)
The Frightened Chameleon (1950)
Mystery Manor (1951)
The Glass Alibi (1952)
The Velvet Mask (1952)
Murder Out of Season (1952)
She Died Laughing (1953)
Murder Mistaken (1953) with Janet Green
The Inverted Crime (1954)
Sally of Scotland Yard (1954) with Geraldine Laws
Death Pays the Piper (1956)
Superintendent Slade Investigates (1956)
Stand In for Murder (1957)
Don't Argue with Death (1959)
Wantons Die Hard (1961)

Resurrected Press Books in A. E. Fielding's *The Chief Inspector Pointer Mystery* Series

RESURRECTED PRESS CLASSIC MYSTERY CATALOGUE

Journeys into Mystery
Travel and Mystery in a More Elegant Time

The Edwardian Detectives
Literary Sleuths of the Edwardian Era

Gems of Mystery
Lost Jewels from a More Elegant Age

Anne Austin
One Drop of Blood
The Black Pigeon
Murder at Bridge

E. C. Bentley
Trent's Last Case: The Woman in Black

Ernest Bramah
Max Carrados Resurrected:
The Detective Stories of Max Carrados

Agatha Christie
The Secret Adversary
The Mysterious Affair at Styles

Octavus Roy Cohen
Midnight

Freeman Wills Croft
The Ponson Case
The Pit Prop Syndicate

J. S. Fletcher
The Herapath Property
The Rayner-Slade Amalgamation
The Chestermarke Instinct
The Paradise Mystery
Dead Men's Money
The Middle of Things
Ravensdene Court
Scarhaven Keep
The Orange-Yellow Diamond
The Middle Temple Murder
The Tallyrand Maxim
The Borough Treasurer
In the Mayor's Parlour
The Saftey Pin

R. Austin Freeman
The Mystery of 31 New Inn from the Dr. Thorndyke Series
John Thorndyke's Cases from the Dr. Thorndyke Series
The Red Thumb Mark from The Dr. Thorndyke Series
The Eye of Osiris from The Dr. Thorndyke Series
A Silent Witness from the Dr. John Thorndyke Series
The Cat's Eye from the Dr. John Thorndyke Series
Helen Vardon's Confession: A Dr. John Thorndyke Story
As a Thief in the Night: A Dr. John Thorndyke Story
Mr. Pottermack's Oversight: A Dr. John Thorndyke Story
Dr. Thorndyke Intervenes: A Dr. John Thorndyke Story
The Singing Bone: The Adventures of Dr. Thorndyke
The Stoneware Monkey: A Dr. John Thorndyke Story
The Great Portrait Mystery, and Other Stories: A Collection of Dr. John Thorndyke and Other Stories
The Penrose Mystery: A Dr. John Thorndyke Story

The Uttermost Farthing: A Savant's Vendetta

Arthur Griffiths
The Passenger From Calais
The Rome Express

Fergus Hume
The Mystery of a Hansom Cab
The Green Mummy
The Silent House
The Secret Passage

Edgar Jepson
The Loudwater Mystery

A. E. W. Mason
At the Villa Rose

A. A. Milne
The Red House Mystery

Baroness Emma Orczy
The Old Man in the Corner

Edgar Allan Poe
The Detective Stories of Edgar Allan Poe

Arthur J. Rees
The Hampstead Mystery
The Shrieking Pit
The Hand In The Dark
The Moon Rock
The Mystery of the Downs

Mary Roberts Rinehart
Sight Unseen and The Confession

Dorothy L. Sayers

Whose Body?

Sir William Magnay
The Hunt Ball Mystery

Mabel and Paul Thorne
The Sheridan Road Mystery

Louis Tracy
The Strange Case of Mortimer Fenley
The Albert Gate Mystery
The Bartlett Mystery
The Postmaster's Daughter
The House of Peril
The Sandling Case: What Would You Have Done?

Charles Edmonds Walk
The Paternoster Ruby

John R. Watson
The Mystery of the Downs
The Hampstead Mystery

Edgar Wallace
The Daffodil Mystery
The Crimson Circle

Carolyn Wells
Vicky Van
The Man Who Fell Through the Earth
In the Onyx Lobby
Raspberry Jam
The Clue
The Room with the Tassels
The Vanishing of Betty Varian
The Mystery Girl
The White Alley
The Curved Blades

Anybody but Anne
The Bride of a Moment
Faulkner's Folly
The Diamond Pin
The Gold Bag
The Mystery of the Sycamore
The Come Back

Raoul Whitfield
Death in a Bowl

And much more!
Visit ResurrectedPress.com
for our complete catalogue

FOREWORD

George Dilnot was a British journalist who became known for his books exploring the history and methods of Scotland Yard, works such as *The Story of Scotland Yard, Scotland Yard: The Methods and Organisation of the Metropolitan Police,* and *Scotland Yard:Its History and Organisation 1829-1929.* He also wrote about celebrated court cases as well as the methods employed by criminals, swindlers, and con men. These books fed a growing public interest in crime, an interest fed by the newspapers of the time who were always willing to publish the details of sensational crimes to boost circulation as well as the cinema whose portrayals of gangsters had caught the public's attention.

Using this background in reporting crime and detection, Dilnot ventured into fiction, producing both a series of mystery novels as well as numerous short stories that appeared in various magazines of the period.

Suspected was published in 1920 at the very beginning of what came to be known as the "Golden Age" of British detective fiction, a period when the who-done-it became the most popular form of fiction, accounting for a quarter of all books published during the era which roughly spanned the period between the two world wars. This was the age of Agatha Christie, Dorothy L. Sayers, Anthony Berkeley, and John Dickson Carr as well as a host of lesser known authors such as Leonard Gribble, Dorothy Fielding, and Elaine Hamilton, all of whom labored ceaselessly to produce mysteries to satisfy the public appetite.

Detective fiction was undergoing a transition at the time *Suspected* came out. The genre, which previously had been dominated by short stories that were long on the puzzle element but short on character development, was shifting over to the mystery novel whose greater length allowed for more emphasis on character interaction and the psychological aspects. While coming up with a clever way to do away with someone was still to be appreciated, it was also important to introduce false clues and red herrings into the mix with the intent of keeping the reader uncertain as to who the real culprit was until the very end, yet all the while "playing fair" by not concealing vital clues.

During the Golden Age, the was also a change in the way the police were portrayed, particularly by the authors of what has been dubbed the "Hum-drum" school of mystery writers. Lest you think this term disparaging, it actually was used by Freeman Wills Croft, the acknowledged master in one of his novels, *The Hogs Back Murder*. In this style of mystery, the police, far from being bumbling incompetents mostly used to introduce humor, are shown as skilled practitioners who solve cases by a combination of hard work and forensic science. In these books, the central detective, rather than being some flamboyant eccentric, is a down to earth sort who succeeds through dogged determination rather than inspiration.

Suspected, as an early example of this style, features as the police detective Inspector Garfield, who works in consort with Jimmie Silverdale, a crime reporter for a London newspaper. As is so often the case with this formula, Inspector Garfield is ably assisted by Detective Sergeant Wade, a brawny specimen only too willing to do the necessary leg work on the case.

The crime itself, involves the murder of a wealthy aeroplane manufacturer who meets his demise at the point of a ladies hat-pin. The complication in the story is that the likely suspect, Hillary Sloane, is the woman that Jimmie Silverdale is in love with. The newspaperman must deal with divided loyalties as he tries to prove the innocence of Sloane.

Dilnot is, unfortunately, not particularly well known these days, either for his non-fiction or his mysteries. It is with pleasure that Resurrected Press offers this new edition of *Suspected* an early Golden Age mystery.

About the Author

George Dilnot (1883-1951) was a journalist and author. He is best known for his non-fiction books about Scotland Yard, famous detectives and celebrated cases and trial. He also wrote over a dozen mysteries and spy thrillers as well as numerous short stories including some in the Sexton Blake series. His series characters include Jim Strang, Inspector Strickland and Horace Elver.

Greg Fowlkes
Editor-In-Chief
Resurrected Press
www.ResurrectedPress.com
www.Facebook.com/ResurrectedPress

I

TWICE in his career had Jimmie Silverdale redoubled three no trumps without the privilege of justifying his confidence. It was the sudden arrival of a Zeppelin bomb that had just put a peremptory end to the rubber on the first occasion. The second time was when Sir Harold Saxon was murdered.

Jimmie was the "crime merchant" of the *Daily Wire*. Crime—in the newspaper sense —was one of the main objects of his existence.

There are distinctions in the newspaper code. For Bill Jones to bludgeon his wife to death in a drunken fit is no crime. It is a venial offense that has no journalistic significance. If the Archbishop of York murdered his cook with his crozier, it would be a crime—more, it would be a "big story."

It would be doing Jimmie Silverdale an injustice to suppose that life held no other interests for him. He viewed the world with a vivacious cynicism tinged with extraordinary enthusiasms. There was for example the girl—but she will find her proper place in this narrative. There was auction bridge and poker. There were books.

He was not beautiful. Untidy, sleek black hair surmounted a hatchet face, and one lock drooped untidily over a sallow forehead. A home-made cigarette clung to his lower lip during his waking hours and he owned a wide-mouthed, irresistible grin. Perhaps it was that grin as much as anything that explained his faculty for collecting friends—queer friends, many of them, but a big asset in his profession.

Through thirty-odd years he had led a variegated life, not without its purple patches. There may have been a strain of Irish blood in his veins, for tight corners were meat and drink to him. They ranged from virtual bankruptcy as the youthful editor-proprietor of a local newspaper to that episode in France where, as an intelligence officer, he had single-handed exterminated a nest of German spies and gained the D.S.O.

Nowadays he had dropped back to the old life on the *Daily Wire*. That journal paid him a thousand pounds a year and held him worth double. Silverdale got results. By what uncanny means he achieved them did not matter. While rival reporters worked tedious and conscientious hours and missed things, Jimmie lounged at the card table of the Paper Club and never "fell down" on a really big story.

He sprawled now, a lanky figure in untidy blue serge, back in his chair and grinned provokingly at the Scotch sub-editor who had doubled his call.

"This is where I've got you hornsnaggered, old lad," he observed. "I'll redouble."

Fate saved the Caledonian. It took the shape of a small boy who burst hurriedly into the room. "You're wanted on the telephone, Mr. Silverdale. Gentleman won't give his name. Says it's most particular and urgent."

Jimmie Silverdale was used to mysterious telephone calls. A short conversation over the wire sent him tearing away in a taxi, utterly forgetful of his unfinished game of bridge. Ten minutes later, he descended at a small tea-room off Piccadilly Circus and greeted a burly red-faced man who was quietly munching toast.

"Cheer-oh, Wing. How goes it?"

"Bearing up, Silver. What are you going to have? Tea?"

The other gave his order and, as the waitress departed, leaned across the table. "What's the game, old bean? You've pulled me away for something else than tea. I'm liable to be peevish, if this is another stumer. You Scotland Yard folk get queer ideas of what a big story should be."

"I've got the goods, Silver. This is a big thing. Ever hear of Sir Harold Saxon?"

"The aeroplane man who pulled a million or so out of the war?"

"That's the lad. He's croaked—done in—murdered!"

Silverdale put down his cup abruptly. He seemed to stiffen in his chair. "Get on with it," he said sharply.

"Big enough for you, eh?" chuckled the other ponderously. "Wait till I've finished. I've only got the bare details of the first report as yet. Nobody knows much of Saxon. He sprang out of nowhere at the beginning of the war—all that is known is that he had spent ten or twelve years in America. He was a capable carpenter and got a job at a small aeroplane factory on the south coast. Somehow he scraped together a few hundred pounds, came to London and bought a disused parish hall. He painted 'Saxon's Aeroplane Works' on it himself, engaged a dozen workpeople and pulled off a bluff at the Ministry of Munitions. Those were the days when aeroplanes were wanted badly. Anyway, by credit, by borrowing, by sheer hard work, he made good. In six months he was employing two hundred hands, in a year two thousand. In two years he was a millionaire and a knight."

Silverdale shifted his position impatiently. "We can dig all this biographical stuff out of the cuttings. Get down to the yarn."

"Sure. I'm coming to it. The Saxon Works are down Wimbledon way. He was popular with everyone, from works manager to the office boy. But about his private history he never said a word, and he has lived for this last couple of years in a flat at St. Ronan's Place. He had one deaf old woman servant who slept in and a maid came in to help her during the day—not that there was much to do for he had most of his meals out.

"Yesterday, this old woman received a wire summoning her to the death-bed of her sister at Bristol. She found her sister well and hearty, and returned to town this morning considerably mystified. She reached the flat at midday and found everything apparently as she left it—until she went into the dining-room. There she saw Saxon tied hand and foot with the curtain hangings, which had been roughly torn down, to a heavy chair.

"His head was sagging on his chest and she thought he had fainted until she tried to arouse him.

"Becoming still more alarmed, as she failed, she rushed out and called a policeman who, after a hasty inspection, summoned a doctor. Then it became clear what had happened. Saxon had been stabbed—stabbed to the heart with a long, thin stiletto-shaped instrument that had been thrust with force up to the hilt. It was, in fact, a woman's hatpin."

Silverdale jotted two or three notes on the back of an envelope. He was beginning to enjoy himself. Yet there was no callousness in his attitude to the murder. It was just a "big" story"—a story that, if he could keep it exclusive to the *Wire*, would ensure heart-burnings and alarms in the dovecots of newspaperland. Perhaps, also, he felt some of the joy of an artist who has a task in hand.

"Good stuff," he commented. "Who's on the job for the Yard?"

"Rack, the divisional man, handled it at first. Our people have sent down Garfield to take charge. What do you make of it, Silver?"

The journalist shrugged his shoulders. He found this detective sergeant from the Scotland Yard Registry useful. It was just a faint possibility that others might also find him useful. Anyway, on a big story, Silverdale would not have trusted his own brother. He shrugged his shoulders.

"Too early to say anything. Where shall I find Garfield?"

"Down at the flat, looking into things. Mind you, Silver, don't let 'em get any hint that you've seen me."

"I 'm not a fool, Wing. And don't forget that I want this to myself for a little."

Wing chuckled. "I get you, Steve," he quoted.

And in a quarter of an hour, Jimmie was slapping a harassed news editor on the back. "Send out an S.O.S. to the printers, laddie. I've got a beat—a peach of a story that'll make your hair curl. In a million happy homes tomorrow our readers will be congratulating themselves on taking the paper that gets the news."

"Cut out the exuberance, Jimmie," growled his superior, trying vainly to rub his injured, back, "and tell me what's biting you."

II

WHENEVER a mysterious crime develops Scotland Yard can usually afford time to organize its net for the confusion of the culprit. Its one aim is detection and arrest. Now a great daily newspaper also organizes, but what it does has to be done swiftly—it must have something to show its readers at breakfast time. It cannot wait. If it holds up a development of news while waiting for a coup it does so at the risk of a rival scoring a "beat."

So Jimmie Silverdale found himself in for a busy evening. Every available man was thrown on to the story. Two dashed out to piece together such details as they might find of Saxon's career. Another was sent to haunt Scotland Yard on the off chance of picking up stray ends of information. A fourth went to Grape Street police station on a similar mission. Still another held himself available to act as general aide to Jimmie. The foreign editor was drafting cables to New York to have Saxon's record investigated in America. The art editor had his minions scouring London for photographs.

Jimmie, his right shoulder hunched over his ear, his hair disheveled, was scrawling in frantic haste a vivid story of the affair so far as he already knew it. A 'sub-editor stood at his elbow and hurried the sheets away as they flashed from under his hand.

The reporter finished, handed the last folio to the waiting sub, and pressed a bell.

"Boy," he yelled impatiently, "get me a taxi."

A lad, catching the feverish excitement which pervades a newspaper office when there is a big story on the move, scurried to the lift. Jimmie slipped into his overcoat and rolled a fresh cigarette.

"We'll move on to St. Ronan's Place, Harry, me lad,"

he said to the man who had been detailed as his assistant. "Perhaps we can nobble Garfield."

There was only one thing in the world that could have diverted Jimmie Silverdale's mind from the work he was engaged upon at that moment. And with the usual perversity of destiny it occurred as he reached the hall door. The commissionaire thrust a letter into his hand.

"Just brought by a district messenger, sir." Jimmie kept his cab waiting while he tore it open. He read it twice and then more slowly and reflectively.

"Dear Mr. Silverdale," it ran.

"You once told me that if ever the time came when I might need your help or advice you would come to me. I need you now. I am in great doubt and distress and know no one other than yourself to whom I can turn. Can you see me immediately? I shall be waiting outside Charing Cross Post Office at seven o'clock. Do come—for God's sake, come!—Hilary Sloane."

The semi-hysterical appeal was as unlike the one girl in the world whom Silverdale hoped might in time be something closer than a friend to him, as it was possible to conceive. It was a couple of years since they had first met in France—she a nurse, he an officer in the intelnce branch, and the acquaintanceship had developed and ripened since the war ended.

Always he remembered her as he first saw her one fragrant spring morning in France. She had stood under a big beech-tree outside the hospital with the sunlight creeping many patterned on to the blue painted ground. All in white she was, and the masses of her soft dark hair framed the dainty oval of her face flushed delicately by good health and open air.

Jimmie, who was a judge, did not fail to mark the personality in the soft curves of the face—, a personality that was emphasized in the-firmly molded chin and the depth of the gray eyes, whether they were alight with mischief or aglow with sympathy with some sufferer broken on the wheel of war.

Of her family, of her pre-war associations he knew little. Their talk had never drifted in that direction and Silverdale was the most incurious person on earth apart from his profession. He knew that she had breeding; he knew that she had nerve—any woman who had faced the red horrors of war as she had done must have nerve.

She lived, a bachelor girl, with a friend somewhere in Chelsea where they shared a studio and dabbled in art. Art, she had told Jimmie once, was her career. Very cleverly, with much gentleness, she had side-tracked him whenever he showed symptoms of falling into the mistake of urging another career upon her—a career that would have necessitated a change of name.

"Don't get sloppy, Jimmie," was her warning, and Jimmie was content to wait.

This, then, was the girl who for some reason had lost her grip on herself sufficiently to send that frenzied appeal for help. Silverdale's brow was puckered with a deep frown as he stepped into the taxi-cab. "I'm going to turn you out at Charing Cross, Harry," he announced. "You'll have to walk down to St. Ronan's Place. Get hold of Garfield if you can and see what you can dig out of him. He's a tight nut but he owes me one or two things and he might give us a line. I'll be with you in twenty minutes or so."

Harry grunted assent. He was a silent man by nature, and Silverdale preferred to have silent assistants on matters of this nature.

At Charing Cross as the cab slowed up they both descended. Jimmie strolled slowly along to the point where he was to meet the girl. Through the crowd he saw her hurrying to meet him, a slim, lithe figure in brown.

"You came, Mr. Silverdale," she exclaimed as she extended her hand. " I knew you would."

He held her hand in his for a moment and a smile flashed across his face. "It used to be Jimmie once. Why this formality?"

A dimple rippled momentarily in her cheek. "Well, Jimmie, if you like. I'm glad you've come." He saw a hint of anxiety in the gray eyes. "You are the one man in the world who can help me now. Where can we go? I want to talk."

"I 've got a taxi here. Come along. No place like a taxi when you want to be absolutely sure you're not overheard." He stood aside to let her take her seat. "I'd like to take you out to dinner but duty forbids. I've got a job on."

She glanced at him quickly, almost apprehensively. "What sort of a job? Has something happened?"

"My dear girl, when one's on a daily paper something's always happening. It's a dog's life anyway. But don't let's talk shop. Get along, driver. Anywhere you like for ten minutes."

He stole a look at her face. She was grave, almost despondent. Her lower lip was quivering though he could see she was making a brave effort to steady herself.

"You've been all shaken up, Hilary," he said. He clasped her small gloved hand in his own and held it tightly. Time was when she would have withdrawn it hurriedly with a laughing reproof. Now she sat still and silent. There were dark rings round her eyes and she was trembling.

"My dear girl! What on earth's the matter?"

She laughed a trifle tremulously. " Nothing is really wrong, but I sent for you because—because—oh, because I wanted a man to give me some advice and I knew you would help."

"Sure!" he agreed.

She pulled her hand away from him. "Oh, Jimmie, you must think me an utter fool. I'm behaving like a school-girl. I can't tell you anything. I know you'll not ask questions. If you'll help me you'll have to do it blindly without trying to find out why. Will you?"

He laughed. "My dear girl, if I didn't know you better

I'd think you were qualifying as a heroine for the moving pictures. What's all this parade of mystery? You can tell me just as much or just as little as you like and I'll do it. I'm not a demonstrative man, Hilary, but you'll believe that I mean it."

As has been said, Jimmie Silverdale was an incurious man in many ways. Yet it cost him something to give that promise. Somehow all the girl's gayety, all her joy in life, all her competent self-possession seemed to have vanished. He longed to take her in his arms as if she were a child to find out what was worrying her and to soothe and comfort her.

Her face showed the relief she felt. "Thank you," she said quietly. "You're a sport, Jimmie. I want you to help me get away out of London—to America for choice, but anyway out of London. I want to go away somewhere where I can't be found—where no one will know where I've gone nor how I've gone. You ought to know how to do it for me."

He stared blankly at her. "You want to go away?"

"Yes. Immediately. No bother about passports or booking passages. Nora Dring and I want to disappear— to vanish from the face of the earth as if we'd never existed. Jimmie"—she clutched at his sleeve—"you must help us. You must. We must get away from London at once—to-night if possible. It is important—vital. You'll do it—Jimmie?"

The man drew a deep breath. "I'll do anything you say, Hilary. But why?"

She held up a warning forefinger. "No questions. You promised."

"Very well," he agreed desperately. "Can you tell me how long you want to be away?"

She shook her head decisively. "I can tell you nothing. If you help you help blind."

"I'm in it," he said with a little gesture of resignation. "I'll go you—blind!"

Impulsively she flung her arms round his neck and

kissed him full upon the lips. Then as if realizing that she
had let her feelings get the better of her she disengaged
herself and a warm flush mantled her face.

For a space there was silence. Jimmie sat looking
straight in front of him as though in deep thought.
Presently he came to himself and glanced at his watch. It
was a sign how deeply he was perturbed that he had
come near committing the newspaper man's cardinal sin.
He had forgotten that he was on a big story. It would
never do to let the paper down.

"Nothing can be done to-night," he said. " I shall be
hard at it till long after midnight. Can you and Miss
Dring be ready to start in the early morning—say seven
o'clock?"

"I'll be ready. Where shall we be going?"

"I don't know. I must think things out. Now get along
home in the taxi and I'll hop out and see after my work.
That has to be done. Good-by for the present."

"At seven o'clock," she repeated and waved him
farewell.

III

HILARY SLOANE was much in Jimmie Silverdale's mind as he made his way to St. Ronan's Place. She had ever seemed to him a girl without the least touch of that feminine lack of balance that for want of a better word is classed as hysteria. Why should she want to vanish?

Whatever was at the back of her mind, it was not triviality. Some great emergency had arisen to change her as she had changed. He had promised to ask no questions but he had not promised not to think.

Was she playing with him? The speculation crossed his mind, though he loyally tried to dismiss it. She had never kissed him before — indeed, she had tried to keep their association on the platonic plane of two chums of the same sex. She had always tried to avoid the intrusion of the attraction of man or woman. Was she playing with him?

"Good heavens — don't I know her well enough to know that she's dead straight?" snarled Jimmie, answering his own thought aloud. "Only a fool would doubt her."

He was approaching the foot of St. Ronan's Place and saw Harry coming towards him. The other reporter shrugged his shoulders as they met. "Nothing doing, Silver. The police are in the flat, but they've got their mouths shut tight as oysters."

"Seen Garfield?" asked Jimmie.

"Can't get near him. Rack came out of the place just now. Very genial and nice when I tackled him, but didn't know anything about any murder. Said he'd just called up to visit a sick friend."

Jimmie chuckled as he rolled a cigarette. The problem of Hilary Sloane had gone for the moment and he was once more a newspaperman on the warpath.

"Like that, is it? They're asses if they think they can keep a story like this sealed up tight. The days of the censor are over. We 've got to get busy. See that board up there?" He pointed to a notice:

WELL-APPOINTED FLATS TO LET
APPLY CARETAKER
NO. 3 ST. RONAN'S PLACE

"What about it?" asked the other blankly.

"This," said Jimmie. " We'll interview that caretaker and see if we can't take a flat for a week or so near that of the late lamented Harold Saxon. It'll be some policeman who'll prevent us going to and fro from our own flat—eh, Harry?"

The interview with the caretaker proved fruitful. For the sum of £20, Jimmie found himself the tenant for a period of two weeks of No. 31b, St. Ronan's Place, and on the opposite side of a corridor was the flat in which still lay the dead body of Harold Saxon.

A plain-clothes police officer was standing at the gate of the lift. He stared blankly at the two journalists. Silverdale smiled on him blandly.

"'Evening, Wade. Mr. Garfield upstairs?"

Wade shrugged his burly shoulders. "I don't know anything, Mr. Silverdale," he protested.

"I'll bet you don't," agreed Jimmie with a grin. "I didn't ask you anything."

"How'd you get on to this, anyway?" asked the other. "We're supposed to have kept the shutters up on this job."

"My dear Watson," said Silverdale mockingly, "the inefficiency of the police force is notorious, even in so simple a matter as keeping close the murder of a munition millionaire. I'm here, as you see. What about it?"

"Cut out the kid stuff," said Wade. "I've heard all about those inefficient police methods. You've got a nose on this kind of thing, Silver, but the guv'nor won't be pleased to see you." He was standing in front of the lift, so that he barred their entrance. "I think on the whole you'd better not butt in for a little while. See?"

"Meaning you're going to prevent us going up!"

"Sorry, old sport. I was told to be particular and see that no one interrupted."

"Do you know I'm a tenant in this block of flats?"

"He's a great little kidder," said Wade, addressing the air. "How long have you been living here, Silver?" he continued genially.

"Go and fetch the caretaker, Harry," said Jimmie. He thrust his hands in his pockets and with legs wide apart whistled cheerfully. Wade surveyed him a little anxiously. He had reason to know Silverdale and he had rarely known him frustrated.

"You don't expect to get by on that bluff, do you?"

"Bluff!" Silverdale was scornful. "You've got another guess coming. I don't bluff. I'm a tenant in these flats, Wade, and a peaceful, law-abiding citizen. These arbitrary police methods don't go down with me as you will find out. Hello—here's the caretaker. Now, my man, tell this gentleman that I'm a tenant in this place. He won't believe me."

"That's so, sir," said the caretaker.

"Well, I'm dodgasted." Wade was staggered and showed it. "Here—my old son—how long has Mr. Silverdale lived here?"

The big moon face of the caretaker looked placidly into the eyes of the detective. Whatever methods Silverdale had employed other than the payment of rent had been thoroughly effective.

"Mr. Silverdale has been a valued tenant of ours for some time," he lied unblushingly.

"That's me," said Jimmie. "Run us up, Wade, like a good fellow since you're acting as engineer-in-chief."

Wade made a grimace, but obeyed.

Silverdale and his colleague made their way into their

new premises and in two minutes had established an observation post from the fanlight of the front door with the aid of a table and kitchen chairs. Watchful waiting was the policy Jimmie had in mind for the moment. While the police were in Saxon's flat, it would be vain to attempt to extract any information from Saxon's housekeeper. Meanwhile, much might be gained by observing the visitors in and out.

Suddenly the door of the opposing flat flung open and a tall jovial-faced man emerged. Jimmie hurriedly descended from his perch, pushed away the table and unlatched the door.

"Come right in, Garfield," he said.

Chief-Detective Inspector Garfield was not the sort of man the average person would have picked on as a disciple of Sherlock Holmes. He had an open, frank, kindly face, and twinkling blue eyes. From his spats upwards, he was a genial, well-dressed, business man. And like most detectives outside the books, he regarded his work as a matter of common sense—common sense and organization.

He held no illusions that he was a romantic figure— few detectives do. Twenty-odd years in the police service do not make a man romantic. Josiah Garfield was hard on occasion, but the twinkle in his eye proved that he was human.

He glanced now from the table to the two journalists and smiled. "Hope I'm not disturbing you?" he apologized.

"Not a bit, not a bit," Jimmie assured him.

The detective closed the door and walked into the dining-room. "I hear you've taken up your quarters here," he said. "Now—getting right down to things—what's the game?"

Silverdale was absorbed in rolling a cigarette. He looked up slowly and his eyes met the detective's. "That's what we want to know," he said. "What are you hiding in there?" He jerked his thumb vaguely in the direction of Saxon's flat. His manner had changed. He was abrupt,

direct. "You know me, Garfield. I'm all out on this yarn.
The story of Sir Harold Saxon's murder will be all over
the world tomorrow. You can't hide your head in the sand
like an ostrich. Do you want me to come in with you? Are
you going to trust me, or shall I pall things off by myself
and perhaps upset the cart?"

Garfield pulled his upper lip thoughtfully. "To tell you
the truth, Jimmie, I'd no idea that you were on the job,
until Wade told me just now. I'm not going to ask how you
got on to this because you wouldn't tell me. I don't trust
newspapermen as a rule, but you're different. We didn't
want too much to leak out till we had got a bit farther.
But I'd sooner have you with me than playing a lone
hand. Is that a bet?"

"We'll call it one," agreed Silverdale.

It is not a usual rule with Scotland Yard men to take
journalists too fully into their confidence, but Garfield
knew what he was doing. Silverdale, working purely in
the interests of his paper, would consider nothing but the
news. It is embarrassing to the detectives when an
avenue of inquiry is revealed prematurely, and Silverdale
had an aptitude for being first.

On the other hand, he knew that Silverdale would
honorably observe an unspoken compact with the police
and act loyally as their ally. It was safer to lay the cards
on the table with such a man.

"Come with me," said Garfield. " Mr. Silverdale won't
be long," he added as he saw Harry show signs of joining
them.

Having thus evaded confiding in a third person, he led
the way to the other flat. The journalist observed a police
photographer busy at work in the dining-room and, with
the detective, moved through to a small interior room.

"This," said Garfield abruptly, "is Velvet Fred, known
to a few other people in the world as Mr. Frederick
Blunt."

Mr. Frederick Blunt was seated in an upright chair,
his wide but well-creased trousers crossed at the knee.

His coat descended in a voluminous skirt well over the waist. His suit had obviously been bought in America. He boasted a small black tooth-brush mustache and a pair of small, restless green eyes that darted to and fro across the room like those of a trapped animal. He showed his white teeth in an animal snarl as the detective spoke. Jimmie could see the veins swell on his white hands as he clenched his fists.

"I'm about fed up with this," he said resentfully. "Haven't you kept me hanging about here long enough? I'm no lackey for the police. If you don't get down to what you want, I'm going to beat it."

Garfield smiled a suave, dangerous smile. "I'm not stopping you, my friend," he observed. "Beat it, by all means. There's the door, if you want to go."

Blunt half rose and reached for the billycock that lay beside his chair. Garfield regarded him steadily, smilingly, and the other seemed to appreciate some subtle menace in his gaze, for he sank back again and twiddled nervously with his hat.

"Mr. Blunt can't tear himself away, you see, Jimmie," went on the detective smoothly. "He's very superstitious, is Mr. Blunt, and perhaps he feels that it might be unlucky. Mr. Blunt and you and I, Jimmie, are going to have a nice, cozy, confidential chat. You see, Mr. Blunt has a great deal up his sleeve that he wants to say to us— haven't you, Mr. Blunt?"

"I didn't croak the stiff," growled Fred.

"So you said before. In his own happy way, Jimmie, Mr. Blunt is saying that he did not murder Sir Harold Saxon. Mr. Blunt is an old friend of mine. That's how I knew where to send for him and why he so courteously responded to my invitation to come here. He couldn't refuse. Mr. Blunt has been a little unfortunate once or twice, but he wouldn't kill an old friend—would you, Fred?"

"Aw—cut out the funny stuff."

"Now," Garfield leaned forward and laid one finger on

the palm of a hand in the manner of a man demonstrating an argument, "our friend denies that he ever knew Saxon. That's a lie, isn't it, Freddie?"

He spoke mildly without any change of voice, and waited for a second for an answer to his challenge. The crook shook his head surlily, roused himself as if to speak and altered his mind.

"It's a lie," went on the chief inspector. "Mr. Blunt knows a great deal about the finger-print system. This flat has been ransacked from top to bottom and finger-prints have been developed on a dozen different things. This tumbler, for instance."

As he spoke, he lifted a tumbler from a side table, he held it up to the light. Drawing a small packet from his waistcoat pocket, he sprinkled a little powder on the side of the glass, blew it away, and showed the sharp detail of thumb and finger marks. Blunt was visibly interested. He leaned forward, his little green eyes fixed apprehensively on the glass.

"That's how it's done," continued Garfield. "I've had photographs taken of finger-prints on other articles and compared with our little collection at the Yard. The gentleman who left his trademark must have paid a visit to this place recently. He'll be lucky if he isn't charged with murder." Suddenly his soft tones changed and his voice rose sternly. "These finger-prints are yours, Freddie. What have you got to say about it?"

An animal growl came from the white lips of the trapped man. In one single swift moment he was on his feet and an automatic appeared as by magic .in his hand. Garfield laughed merrily and flung his huge bulk face forward on the ground. Jimmie leapt aside and then towards Blunt, but quick as he was the detective was quicker.

As he dropped, Garfield's right hand whipped out and caught Freddie by the ankle. A quick jerk threw him off his balance and he fell heavily, the pistol flying from his hand. Jimmie pounced upon it, but before he could recover himself, Blunt was free and was coming at him with dynamic fury.

One never knows what a man will do in an emergency. Freddie Blunt was a scoundrel, but among those who knew him best at Scotland Yard, he was not reckoned an apostle of physical violence. Garfield had, however, roused him beyond all reasoning. He saw the shadow of the gallows before him and to avoid it, he was willing to fight in a blind frenzy.

With blazing eyes he tore at Silverdale. The journalist was hurled aside and staggered against the wall, still grasping the automatic. Garfield was on his feet once again and his muscular hands fastened themselves at the mad-man's neck. Almost without effort, he lifted the squirming ruffian clean from the floor and held him for a second while he made sure of his grip. Then he flung him heavily across the room.

"Lie there, you rat!"

Under the stress of physical conflict, primitive man had flowed out in the usually self-controlled detective for once, but his self-possession returned almost instantly. Not so with Blunt. He lay where he had fallen, breathing heavily, his green eyes flashing from one to the other. Half a dozen men of the corps of detectives who were engaged in various investigations in the flat had clustered round the door. Garfield dismissed them with a gesture.

"That's all right," he said coolly. "Somebody very nearly got hurt, but it's all right now. Now, Velvet," he continued, as his subordinates disappeared, "you can get up if you're tired of making a fool of yourself." He brushed the dust from his clothes with a handkerchief fastidiously. "You don't think I was thinking you committed this murder, do you?" A slight touch of contempt crept into his voice. "You haven't nerve enough."

Blunt picked himself up sulkily. "What were you driving at, anyway?"

Silverdale intervened for the first time. His voice was as silky as Garfield's and he swung the automatic idly to and fro by the trigger guard.

"What Mr. Garfield is driving at, if I'm not making any mistake," he said, "is that if you didn't kill this man yourself, you have a very good suspicion who did!"

Blunt knotted his hands sulkily. The gaze of both men was fixed on him steadily. "I don't know," he answered with a note of doggedness in his voice.

Jimmie shrugged his shoulders and glanced interrogatively at the inspector. Garfield nodded. He was content to let the journalist try by methods that had before then been successful with German prisoners.

The journalist thrust his head forward and stared straight between Blunt's eyes. "You do know," he rasped.

"What were you doing in this flat?" broke in Garfield. "Who sent you? What did you want?"

"Let me alone," protested Blunt. "I wasn't in the flat. I don't know."

They plied him pitilessly, brutally, with a ceaseless rain of questions. Like some dogged animal, he held them at bay as they alternately threatened and coaxed. There' is no third degree in Britain, and, technically, both of his questioners knew they were infringing the strict letter of the law. But many crimes would go unsolved if the limits of legality were always observed in these cases.

Garfield apparently gave it up at last. "That's enough," he growled.

"There's only one thing that makes you unwilling to talk," said Jimmie. "You were in the flat. If you didn't kill Sir Harold Saxon, who did?"

White and shaken, Blunt shook his head dumbly.

"You're right, Jimmie," agreed Garfield. "Once for all, Freddie, listen to me. I know you didn't kill this man. Now unless you cough up your story—it's between friends now—I swear I'll let you go down to prove you didn't. Get me?"

"You mean you'll charge me with the murder?"

"I'll do that," said Garfield, nodding with grim emphasis.

There was method in this terrorization. Garfield knew he was dealing with a man who was beyond the fringe of decent human society. That Velvet Fred held the thread of the mystery, he was convinced and it needed little reasoning to see that some strong object was keeping his lips sealed. A stronger motive was needed to make him speak.

Even for Garfield, it was carrying things close to the bone to threaten to accuse a man he knew to be innocent of a capital crime. But he saw no other means of forcing the crook's hand. Once in the dock, Velvet Fred would have to reveal his story or run the risk of being hanged. Blunt was no fool. Kightly or wrongly, he believed that Garfield meant his threat. He went very white.

"I'll tell you," he said in a low voice.

"The straight goods, now. No lies."

"I'll give you the straight goods. Look here, Mr. Garfield, it's up to you to see that I come out of this with my skin safe. If Eston—"

Garfield interrupted with a low whistle. "So Eston is mixed up in this. Don't you worry—I'll look after you. Half a moment. We'll have your statement in writing."

He summoned one of his aides, who placed himself with notebook and pencil at a low table. "Head this: 'The voluntary statement of Frederick Blunt, otherwise'— there's nothing to smile at, Silver. This is a deadly serious business."

"I'm not smiling," protested Jimmie.

"Right-oh. Now we're ready, Velvet. Go ahead!"

"There isn't much to it, Mr. Garfield, but you know Eston. He'll have me, if it's twenty years hence."

"Who's Eston?" interrupted Jimmie.

"Eston," explained Garfield, "is the biggest crook in London—perhaps in the world. I'll tell you more about him when Velvet has finished."

"Well, I met Eston a week ago at a restaurant up

Regent Street way. He was with a bird—"

"A girl?"

"I said so," said Blunt aggrievedly. "They were having a bit of an argument and didn't take any notice of me for a bit. Presently the girl went and Eston beckoned me over.

"'Can you do a little job for me—or rather for a lady?' he asks.

"'Sure,' said I, 'if there's anything in it for me.'

"Then he tells me that there's some papers in this flat and that he's bound to have 'em. He offered me fifty of the best and I took on the job. I pulled it off night before last. The gink who lives here had a safe that you'd laugh to see."

"The safe here has not been tampered with," said Garfield.

"Hasn't it?" said Velvet scornfully. "Give me five minutes with the combination and I'll lock and unlock it any time you want. Anyway, I did it—got the papers—a bundle of letters—and handed 'em to Eston."

"Was the girl there then?"

"Sure. It was at the same restaurant. She was seated at a different table, but Eston went over with the goods after he finished with me."

"You'd recognize her again?"

"I think so."

"Then look at this."

Garfield pulled a cabinet photograph from his pocket and thrust it in front of the crook. Velvet nodded his head. "That's the lady."

"That's the woman who killed Harold Saxon," said Garfield, handing the picture over to Silverdale.

Jimmie only needed one glance. The room reeled round him.

For the portrait was that of Hilary Sloane.

IV

THERE are overwhelming moments of catastrophe which, for a time, deaden the faculties and then leave them preternaturally acute. Silverdale was stunned—but only for an instant. He sought vainly in his mind for some outlet to the tangle. What was Hilary Sloane doing in this galley?

Saxon had been killed by a hatpin—evidence of probability, though not of certainty, that the person who killed him was a woman. Then her frantic appeal to him to get her away from London, to enable her to disappear. To his logical mind the motive stood out now sun-clear. The links bringing home the crime to her were all connected. Her meeting with Eston, her photograph in the flat, the hatpin, her anxiety to vanish.

And yet—and yet! Intuition which he vainly tried to dismiss as mere sentiment told him he was wrong. This sunny girl, this woman whom he had set on a pinnacle in his soul—a murderess! It was impossible!

"What's the matter, Jimmie?" Garfield's suave voice broke in on him as from a great distance. "You don't know the lady, do you?"

Silverdale pulled himself together, though for a perceptible second he hesitated.

"Lord, no! She's some looker, isn't she?" The casual words stuck in his throat.

"A good-looking girl," agreed the inspector. "We've got to get hold of her. You don't know her, I suppose, Velvet?"

The crook had been surveying Silverdale narrowly. His scrutiny dropped and he shook his head.

"Never seen her in my life before I ran across her with Eston, Mr. Garfield."

"Not the slightest idea where she is?"

"Not the ghost of a glimmer."

"Right you are, Velvet. Sign your name to your statement and you can go. But mind you," Garfield emphasized his warning with upraised forefinger, "you'll be wanted again. No tricks now. Understand?"

"Sure, I get you. I'll not double-cross you. Stand on me. Good-night, Mr. Garfield. Goodnight, Mr. Silverdale."

He picked up his hat, brushed it with his arm and moved jauntily out. Silverdale was thankful for the respite. Rightly or wrongly, with that lie to the detective he had committed himself to a course of action. His duty to his paper, his moral obligation to Garfield, the ethical duty of every citizen to see justice done, he had sunk fathoms deep. A pair of dancing gray eyes were more to him than all the world. At all costs Hilary Sloane must be protected.

"A nice gentleman, Mr. Blunt," he commented smilingly.

"Glad you like him," said Garfield. "Well, Jimmie, I expect that will be all the show for to-night, though we never can tell. We'll be all out after Eston for a while— and then the girl."

"Ah, yes, the girl," Silverdale moistened his dry lips. "Who is she?"

"That's what we've got to find out," said Garfield. "Now if you like, I'll show you over the flat, tell you what we've done and then home to bed." He yawned. "Heigh-ho, I'm tired."

Even the apprehension that weighted him like a pall could not lessen Jimmie's vivid professional interest in the details of the crime. His memory on what he saw or was told was as infallible as a cash-register. Small things may mean much in detective or newspaper work, though it is not always so simple to know which, of a hundred trivialities may be the one of moment. He listened, observed, and questioned, but nothing served to shake the obvious horrible fact that oppressed him.

He found Harry waiting for him impatiently when at

last he had said good-night to Garfield and shook off his colleague's questioning with, an unusual surliness. He wanted to think.

In spite of Garfield's assurance that nothing farther could happen that night, he was not easy. The unexpected frequently happens with amazing suddenness on criminal investigations. The ponderous machine of Scotland Yard was at work at full pressure and Silverdale, though he knew its limitations, also knew its immense ramifications. Men were probably raking out Saxon's history for a score of years past, both in Britain and the United States. The hounds were out after Eston—he had no doubt that general instructions had been flashed by wire to every police district—in every port, at every railway station, there would be quiet, alert men in and out of uniform, watching and ready. There would be the direct pursuit, organized by Garfield himself. The organization of Scotland Yard and its allies is beyond doubt wonderful. No man whose identity is known—and Eston's was known—can hope to evade it. When Eston was caught—what then?

Fort, the news-editor, met them in the corridor as they reached the *Daily Wire* office. He was in his shirt-sleeves.

"Back again, Silver. What luck?"

"I've got all the facts up to now, Fort," said Silverdale. "But I don't know how far to go. It may be that this won't be the big story I thought."

"Listen to him," Fort admonished the ceiling. Then he punched his desk with his fist. "You know as well, or better than I do, Jimmie, that it's a big story. Let's talk sense. How have you got on? There's a woman in it, so Laughton, who's been up to the Yard, tells me. Have they got on to her? Have you got a photograph?"

Silverdale laughed happily, but the merriment was solely for the benefit of the other. A photograph of Hilary Sloane was in his pocket at that moment. No power on earth could have induced him to surrender that picture to be reproduced for all the world to gaze at. The caption that would have gone beneath it burned in his brain. "Suspected!—Hilary Sloane, who is wanted for the murder of Sir Harold Saxon."

Yet outwardly he was a man entirely at ease. "Photograph," he repeated. "You'll have to wait for that, Fort. I can't do miracles. How's the other stuff coming in?"

"Nothing startling. Just good, ordinary stuff. We can't expect much till to-morrow." Fort was relieved to see Jimmie taking a more normal interest in affairs. "Better make a start, old lad, and get the final story into shape for the last edition, hadn't you?"

"Perhaps you're right," agreed Silverdale. He jumped from his seat on the table, yawned and stretched himself. "Looks as if I might have a stiff day to-morrow. I'll finish up, go home, and have a good sleep. I'm a bit overtired."

There was one matter that Jimmie had to attend to before he got down to the story. In the privacy of a telephone box, he put through a call to a garage which had helped both him and the *Daily Wire* before.

"I want a car outside Sloane Street Underground Station at seven in the morning," he said. "Something good. None of your broken-winded antiques. Get that? I may want to drive myself and I don't know how long I shall need it."

Jimmie wrote more slowly than his usual feverish speed that night. Every word he considered with care. Whatever might befall in the hours and days to come, he was determined that Hilary Sloane's name should not be dragged in the mire. A hundred keen eyes in Fleet Street he knew would scrutinize his story of the crime in the morning. Men would be seeking for a hint, a clew, some line of investigation. He did not want that line to lead to Hilary Sloane.

V

THE building was quivering with the shuddering rumble of the great printing presses in the basement as Jimmie Silverdale quitted the *Daily Wire* office. He shivered as the cool fresh air of the early morning struck him and buttoned his thin raincoat tightly. Always it had seemed to him there was something unreal, unnatural, in the noisy activity of the streets of newspaperdom at that hour. Now, somehow, it jarred upon him more than ever.

As he turned into Fleet Street, he glanced at his watch. It was two o'clock. Only by great luck could he hope to pick up a nocturnal taxicab. He quickened his stride and moved westward. After all, it was but a walk to Chelsea. Mrs. Grundy and the conventions might go hang. He would see Hilary. He felt chilled. The exercise would warm him.

Now it would be doing Jimmie Silverdale an injustice to suppose that he had usually held any diffidence in pursuing a course he had marked out. He considered difficulties as they arose. He set out on that journey with the fixed intention of rousing Hilary from bed—if she had gone to bed, which he doubted—and having the whole subject thrashed out. There was no time for finesse and it was no occasion for tact. She was suspected of a murderous crime and, if innocent, he must have her version of the story if he was to aid her. If guilty— He tried to put the thought away as black treason. Yet reason fought down sentiment. Why!—why!—why? The word hammered through his brain with every beat of his footsteps on the pavement.

At Sloane Square he wavered. Neither morally nor physically was he a coward, yet he. could not bring himself to face Hilary Sloane at that unwonted hour with the question that, however he framed it, must be an accusation. No, he would wait until their appointment at seven o'clock.

Smoking innumerable cigarettes, he paced the deserted streets till after dawn, pausing only once at a stall to drink some steaming decoction which, by sheer imagination, might be called coffee. At five minutes to seven, he pressed the bell at Hilary's flat.

She answered the door herself, fully dressed, and his keen eyes sought her face for some sign of the tortured night he knew she must have passed. But there was no sign there. A pink flush was in her cheeks, her eyes were sparkling. She looked entirely at ease.

"Come in, Jimmie," she said buoyantly. "You're punctual. Been sitting up all night to make sure of being on time?"

"Something of the sort," he agreed. And then dryly: "You seem brighter than when I saw you last night."

"My dear Jimmie!" she laughed. "I had the mopes last night. I don't know what was wrong with me. But as soon as I placed matters in your competent hands, I knew that everything would be all right, of course." She dragged him by the arm forward. "Here, get your coat off and come and have some breakfast. Nora is having hers in her room. She's a lazy creature. We'll be able to have a quiet talk. Don't look at me like that. What's the matter?"

Her apparent light-heartedness took Jimmie unawares. Women were past all understanding. Was this chatter, this brightness—a pose? If so, she was a consummate actress.

"Nothing wrong with me," he said slowly. "I've been thinking."

"Fatal. Break yourself of it at once, or it'll get hold of you like the dope business. Laugh. —that's the only thing—laugh."

They had reached the little breakfast-room and she was busy with eggs and coffee. Her manner had to some extent relieved his mind, though why or how he might have been at a loss to explain. She seemed determined to carry things off in a matter-of-fact way. There was none of that strained embarrassment on her side which he had expected at their meeting.

He ate and drank mechanically, silent and thoughtful, while she talked gayly on, never referring to the object of his visit even indirectly. He was trying to catch a serious note beneath her flippancy and not succeeding.

"I'm damned if I can make it all out," he said in a sudden access of irritability, pushing his cup away and rising from the table. "What's the game, Hilary?"

She looked up, startled, apprehensive. "Good heavens, Jimmie, you startled me. I thought you'd broken my pet breakfast set. I thought you were a man who never suffered from nerves." She crossed the room and laid a slim hand, light as a feather, on his arm. Her touch seemed to electrify him and he caught her other hand.

"Let's have done with all this fencing. I want to know things. I want you to trust me."

A thin pucker showed in her forehead and she disengaged herself gently. "Don't be melodramatic," she murmured. "You're behaving a little bit like an idiot, Jimmie. Did you know it?"

He choked back an expression used in moments of stress by the Army in Flanders. Her self-possession staggered him.

"I am an idiot," he said bitterly. "No one but an idiot would have given you the promise I made last night."

At last there was a change. All the light had gone from her face and she was grave. "You're not going back on that, Jimmie? You are going to help us out of town?"

He saw relief in the gray eyes as he nodded. "Yes; I'll help," he said quietly.

"Then you mean that you're sorry you promised to ask no questions," she went on. "Whatever you say or do, I'm going to hold you to that. That's why I've been talking about everything else under the sun. If you've made things all right for us to get away, I'm content. I want to know no more nor think any more about it. I'm content to leave everything in your hands."

He stood, one elbow on the mantelpiece, looking down on her with calculating gaze. She had cleared a space on the table and sat idly swinging her feet to and fro. A dainty picture she made and there was no suggestion of drama in her attitude or tone.

"That's rather clever," said Silverdale admiringly. "You want to put me on my honor not to know too much."

She glanced down at her gray woolen stockings and nodded. A slight flush had crept into her cheek.

"I'd do much for you, Hilary," he went on. "You know how I have felt, how I still feel, about you." She gave a slight shrug of impatience and he went on. "I'll leave that out then. When I gave you my promise, I felt whatever your reasons were for wishing to leave London in so extraordinary a manner, they were your own private affairs and I had no right to pry. Since I last saw you circumstances have changed. I don't believe you can carry this through on a lone hand. Let me come in."

She swung herself impulsively from the table and seized both his hands, pulled him out into the room and danced half round him.

"You're a bright boy, Jimmie, and a clever boy, but you're dazzled by your own cleverness sometimes. It wants a woman to run this show properly, and I'm going to be in command. Just for once, I'm going to run you in blinkers to see how it feels."

"One moment, Hilary. Do you realize the danger?"

"Danger?"

"Yes. Perhaps I understand more easily than you credit. I know more than you think, Hilary. I tell you that you stand in the greatest peril that man or woman can stand in. What may happen—God knows what may happen! It turns my blood cold to contemplate. You have brains, you have courage, but you are a woman."

"If I didn't know you, Jimmie Silverdale, I should say you had gone raving mad. This is getting curiouser and curiouser, as Alice in Wonderland said. Can't you be plain?"

"I'll be plain then, my dear. You have asked me to help you—in blinkers. Well, something—not my own will—has removed the blinkers. I have seen—I have heard—"

"What?" she snapped the question out defiantly.

He caught her by the wrist. "Have you ever heard of Harold Saxon?"

"I don't know. I may have. I can't say. Let me go. You are hurting me!"

He released her. "Harold Saxon was the head of the Saxon Aeroplane Works. He was killed yesterday before you sent that frantic note to me. He was stabbed with a woman's hatpin."

She stood as though frozen to stone. Her eyes were fixed on his face, searching apprehensively. "What has that to do with me?" she asked and he could see her lips were dry.

"It has everything to do with you. You have told me you didn't know Saxon. At any rate he knew you. There was a photograph of you in his possession at the time of his death. The detectives are linking up evidence, that will associate you with the crime. They are looking for you, Hilary. You are trying to leave London."

"Oh!"

The cry was so faint that he scarcely heard it. She held her arms out towards him and then they dropped to her side. Slowly her feet seemed to fail under her. Hilary Sloane, whose nerve had never failed under the most terrible conditions in the blood-soaked hospitals in France, for the first time in her life had unobtrusively fainted.

The door opened. A slim, yellow-haired girl with pale complexion and in traveling dress entered with outstretched hand.

"Good-morning, Mr. Silverdale. Why, what's the matter with Hilary?"

"Fainted, I think," said Jimmie. "She didn't seem quite herself when I came in."

VI

NORA DRING moved swiftly to where Hilary was lying and lifted her head. "What have you been saying to her?" she demanded angrily.

Before Silverdale could reply, Hilary opened her eyes. "Silly of me to do that," she said. "I'm all right. Don't begin to fuss me."

As a proof she sat upright, tailor fashion, and her hands flew to her hair which she began to pat and rearrange. Then she accepted Silverdale's aid to rise and clung to him a little unsteadily. Nora Dring was regarding her earnestly. "What happened?" she asked.

"I don't know," said Hilary. "I was talking to Mr. Silverdale and—and—I just dropped. I'm perfectly fit now."

"H'm!" Nora's gaze shifted to the journalist. He met it with bland unconcern.

"A car has been waiting outside Sloane Street Station for some little time," he said. "I thought it wiser that I should drive it here and pick you up. Now if you ladies are ready?"

"Will you arrange about getting the luggage down, dear?" said Hilary to Nora, "I've just got to put my hat on."

The yellow-haired girl lifted her shoulders as though disclaiming all responsibility for some situation that she only guessed at. Another question trembled on her lips, but was never spoken. With another shrug she left the room.

Hilary supported herself with her hand on a chair.

"Jimmie," she said, with a quiver in her voice. "You don't think—that?"

"I think nothing, Hilary. I am just telling you the

facts."

"But you—oh, my God!" She buried her face in her hands and seemed to be fighting for her self-control. "I tell you I know nothing—nothing! I have never seen Saxon in my life. It is preposterous. Oh, Jimmie, I shall go mad! You believe me, don't you? Nora will be back in a moment." She sprang forward and caught his hands passionately in hers. "Say you believe me!"

A thousand questions thronged to his lips, but he resolutely repressed them. There would be time and opportunity later. Reason fought with intuition. The facts were against her, but his instinct told him that she was playing no part. Suddenly he caught her roughly to his breast and kissed her.

"I believe you, Hilary," he said hoarsely. "I'll do what I can. Whatever it costs, you can count on me."

It has been said before in this narrative that Silverdale was not given to demonstrative emotion. Yet for once he had permitted himself to be carried away. His brain was coldly clear and he realized whither he might be led. He had few illusions as to the ultimate certainty of Scotland Yard finding out his association with Hilary Sloane. Then—well, that contingency could be faced when it arose.

As Nora Dring returned she found two very casual people in the dining-room. "Not ready yet, Hilary?"

"I'll be with you in a minute," said Hilary, and literally true to her word it was less than a minute before she was back. "Where are we going?" she asked.

"First of all to Paddington. Then you will go to a village in Berkshire where an aunt of mine lives. She will be only too willing for you to stay there, till I can fix. up some more definite plan."

As Silverdale walked round to fetch the car, he had an uneasy sense of being watched which he could not shake off. He tried all the tricks which he knew to find out whether this was actually so. He loitered before shop windows, he turned suddenly on his heel and walked in a reverse direction, he turned corners and came to a quick halt, but no pursuer fell into these traps. He decided that he was suffering from nerves.

A green car was waiting outside Sloane Square. "I'm Mr. Silverdale," explained Jimmie to the driver. "I'll handle this car myself. You might meet me in Piccadilly Circus in an hour's time in case I want you."'

Jimmie took his seat at the steering-wheel. Then an idea occurred to him and he artistically dropped a rug so that it obscured the rear number of the car. One never lost anything through precaution.

He found the girls waiting for him at the flat and to his regret Miss Dring took the vacant seat by his side and Hilary had the body of the car to herself.

"You must think all this very mysterious, Mr. Silverdale," she commented as he started. "Hilary is a queer girl. It is awfully good of you to humor her."

"I am only too glad to be of service," said Jimmie formally. "Hell! what was that?"

There was a shout behind them and, with a hasty glimpse over his shoulder, the reporter caught sight of men running.

Nora Dring gave a quick moan. "Who are they? They will get us."

Jimmie did not know who the men might be, but he had a good suspicion and was taking no chances. The car leapt forward and took a corner, as it seemed, on two wheels. In defiance of all speed limits he let her have full power. Luckily there was little traffic in the streets. For half a mile he held on recklessly and then slowed to a more reasonable pace.

"We've shaken them off. There's no sense in calling attention to ourselves," he said.

It was close on five-and-twenty past eight when they reached Paddington. Jimmie summoned a porter and shook hands with the two girls.

"I'll not come to the platform," he said. "Good-by and good-luck. If you have any letters to write, send them to me. I'll post them off. Understand?"

"Good-by and thank you," said Hilary—in a low voice.

As he waved them off, he was alert to anything that might happen about him. That alarm as they had started from Chelsea showed that the flight had been undertaken only just in time —if in time. It was as well that he had taken precautions. The car could not be identified by its number anyway, and the fact that he had driven himself closed an avenue of inquiry that would certainly be taken up. His wandering eye rested for a second on the backs of the two girls, now half a dozen paces away. He froze into immobility and his stare became fixed until they passed beyond sight. A smothered exclamation came from his lips.

"Good God! What a blundering blind ass I am. I wonder if—"

Slowly and thoughtfully he wheeled the car round and glided out. As he took the corner outside the station a slim young man of perhaps between thirty and thirty-five slipped hurriedly into the roadway and held up his hand.

"Just got 'em off in time," muttered Silverdale "beneath his breath. "I don't know this chap, but he's on the job all right." He pulled up.

"Mr. Silverdale?" questioned his interrupter smoothly.

"Further deception is useless," agreed Jimmie with a wide-mouthed grin. He studied his interlocutor closely. Now, on nearer approach, he was not so certain of the man's age. The face that looked into his with smiling good humor was a strong one. Pale blue eyes, high cheek bones, and a mouth like a rat-trap, were surmounted by a head of corn-colored hair. He was dressed in a dark brown suit that bore the stamp of a West-End tailor. He had removed his hat with a somewhat foreign gesture as he spoke.

"You will pardon my apparent impertinence," he said, speaking in a quiet, self-possessed voice. "I believe you have just left two ladies at the station. I am interested in them."

Jimmie relinquished the wheel and began to roll a cigarette. He was apparently very engrossed in the process for he did not answer for some little while. He glanced at the stranger from under lowered lids.

"I'd hate to deceive you," he said gently. "I have been on a joy-ride and I have had no ladies in this car. You are under a misapprehension, sir."

A hint of amusement crept into the cold eyes. "If it entertains you to tell a fatuous lie, Mr. Silverdale, don't mind me. I have been at considerable trouble to come here to meet you and I know a very great deal." He placed one highly polished boot on the running-board and gesticulated gently with a gloved forefinger. "That will be obvious to you from the fact that I am here."

Silverdale refused to be impressed. "Continue. You interest me strangely," he laughed.

The stranger bit his lip a trifle irritably. The mockery was not lost on him. Then he laughed. "I understand. You are trying to make me lose my temper. It is always good to make the other man angry. But be careful, Mr. Silverdale. I know you have just smuggled Miss Sloane and Miss Dring out of town. What's more—I know why."

Silverdale was conscious of a keen scrutiny as the last words were flung at him. He held an attitude of indolent detached amusement. "My dear Sherlock—" he protested.

"Suppose you drop that pose," suggested the other. "Let's get down to business. Tell me—" he pulled himself fully on to the running-board closer to the journalist and dropped his voice—"on which side of the fence are you?"

"Let's see," said Jimmie casually. "Is there a fence!"

"You're playing a dangerous game, young man. You can't fool with me. I want to know where you stand. You can be useful to me. You are in the confidence of the police. If you want to make a fortune—if you want to marry Hilary Sloane—you will come in on my side."

Silverdale's fists were clenching and unclenching nervously. There was none of that ironical banter in his voice when he next spoke.

"You—Eston. I'd see you burn first."

"You know me?"

"I've known you for the last five minutes. If you're not out of my sight in a matter of seconds—do you see that policeman over there?" He jerked his thumb over his shoulder.

"Oh, no," Eston shook his head. "You wouldn't do that, Mr. Silverdale. As you so charmingly put it a moment ago, you'd be willing enough to see me burn, but I very much doubt if you'd be so willing to see Hilary Sloane — ha!"

He reeled back as Silverdale's fist caught him full in the face and staggered his full length on the pavement. He recovered himself like a wildcat and came back. A sheen of blue revealed itself in his right hand and Silverdale faced the business end of an automatic pistol.

He leaned back carelessly. "That's the stuff, Mr. Eston. Shoot away!"

Eston grunted. Then as though recalled to a realization of his position, he pocketed the weapon. "We'll see about this," he snarled. "I've not finished with you yet, Mr. Silverdale."

And turning on his heel, he walked swiftly away.

VII

INSPECTOR GARFIELD Sorted his correspondence and, sitting on a high stool, ran through the reports and statements which began the *dossier* of the Saxon case with some impatience. At a footstep behind him, he failed to turn his head.

"Out of it," he ordered peremptorily. "Come back in five minutes. Can't you see I'm busy?"

"That's too bad," said a quiet voice. Garfield wheeled round sharply, nearly overbalancing his tall stool.

"I beg your pardon, Sir Richard. I didn't know it was you."

Sir Richard Essex, Assistant-Commissioner of the Metropolitan Police, laughed. A quiet, unostentatious man whose tastes ran rather in the direction of literature than of crime, he had brought the Criminal Investigation Department to a high state of efficiency by methods that were felt rather than seen. He picked up a square of mirror from Garfield's desk and adjusted his tie. It was like him to walk in casually rather than send for his subordinate as other administrative officials might have done.

"I hate to disturb you, Garfield," he said mildly. "I wanted to hear how things were going."

"You've seen the reports, Sir Richard."

"I've seen the reports. That isn't exactly the same thing." He placed the mirror gently back in place. "You've heard of this affair at Chelsea?"

"I haven't been in five minutes. Has anything gone wrong?"

Essex shrugged his shoulders. "You put a couple of men on to shadow your friend Velvet when you finished with him last night."

"Yes. A mere matter of precaution."

"I've heard some of your colleagues call you lucky Garfield. Other people have described you as a genius. You have Velvet followed, 'as a mere matter of precaution,' and he leads you clean to the heart of the mystery, saving hours, and perhaps days, of tedious heartbreaking investigation. Do you know he went straight off to Eston after he left you?"

Garfield drummed on his desk. "I might have guessed," he said thoughtfully. "Velvet's fifty different types of a dirty gutter-rat and he'd not hesitate at a double-cross. He wants to run with the hare and hunt with the hounds. But I suppose we got Eston!"

"Oh, no. They met at a night club and our men weren't very sure of Eston—though I have no doubt from their description that he was the other. Our chaps smuggled themselves in and witnessed a long conversation between the two, though they could not hear what was said. Even if they had been sure of Eston they had no instructions. You had told them to hang on to Velvet."

"If they'd used their brains," grumbled Garfield, striding nervously across the room, "they'd have taken a chance. You can work till you're sore on this kind of job and never get anywhere unless you're willing to take a chance. There's not a chief in the service who hasn't risked his career on a chance, time and again, as you know, sir. You can't catch criminals with red tape. We may be a year before Eston gives us another opportunity. I'll tell those lads—"

"A little advice from you won't do 'em any harm," agreed the Assistant-Commissioner dryly. "Well, Eston and Velvet were joined by a third man, and presently the two latter left together. They spent the night at a small hotel off the Strand and left early this morning by Underground to Sloane Square. Our chaps hung on to them and followed them to a quiet street in Chelsea where most of the flats are used as artists' studios. Velvet went inside one of the buildings, while his friend kept watch outside. Ten minutes later he came out, walked to Sloane Square and telephoned to someone."

Garfield wrinkled his brows thoughtfully. "Now I wonder what he had picked up there?" he said.

"Lord knows. I'm giving you the story. He came back and hung about. A little later, from the same block of buildings, there came a newspaper chap—a man you know, I think—named Silverdale. Our men know him well."

"Jimmie Silverdale—the *Daily Wire* man?"

"That's he. He went away, returned in a little, driving a green motor-car with the number obscured and two women—girls—got in with a quantity of luggage. He drove off instantly and Velvet and his pal, who were lurking in the opposite direction—were after it. Then one of our chaps recognized one of the girls in the car and made a dive."

Garfield thrust his hands deep in his trousers pockets and came to a halt, facing his chief. "The woman!" he exclaimed. "The girl whose photograph was found in Saxon's flat?"

"That's the lady. Our people hiked after her like hounds, by their account, but Silverdale drove like a madman. They got clean away."

"A pretty mess they seem to have made of it," observed Garfield contemptuously. "But if Silverdale was in it," he went on, "we'll be knowing more about it soon. He's evidently struck some line that we didn't know of and gone straight for the girl. He 'll play the game, will Silverdale. He won't hold anything out on us."

"Why should he spirit them away, though?"

The chief inspector's eyes twinkled. "A newspaperman on a big story doesn't like to be caught napping. He's taken this lady beyond reach of any other journalist—in case of accidents. Somehow he's introduced himself to her and by some persuasion—it may be money or it may be some other influence—he's got her out of reach of his fellow hawks of Fleet Street. What happened to Velvet?"

"No one knows. He cleared out in the confusion. Our men went round to the studio and made a few inquiries. There were two girls living there—one named Nora Dring. But the one we want is an artist who was a Red Cross nurse during the war—a girl named Hilary Sloane."

"It looks like being a pretty full day," said Garfield. "Will you come down to this place where Miss Hilary Sloane hung out, sir?"

"I was going to suggest it. When will you be ready to start?"

"In half an hour. I have a lot of odds and ends to clear up." Garfield turned again to his *dossier*.

There he read in a detailed report from Summerfield—the senior of the two men who had been told off to shadow Velvet—all that the assistant-commissioner had told him. It took him less than five minutes to summon that individual and his colleague and to scorch them in a brief, but exhaustive, review of their capacity and common-sense. He dismissed them with their tails—so to speak—between their legs and sent them with Wade, his most trusted aide, down to Chelsea to watch the studio and await his coming.

He was, as he had said, easy in his mind about Silverdale and he mentally congratulated himself on his good sense in making an ally of that enterprising journalist. No suspicion that Jimmie might have any more intimate association with the central figure in the case than that as a journalist occurred to him. Silverdale would not break his compact to work hand in hand with the police.

Garfield like all good detectives had something in common with the good journalist. He had no pretensions to omniscience but he did know where to gather his information. The microscope was not his province, but he always knew how to lay his hand on an expert from a fountain-pen manufacturer to a gunsmith. The trail on any crime is largely a matter of expert witnesses. They, alone can swear to facts—and facts are the only thing that convict in Anglo-Saxon courts of justice.

There was, for instance, the stiletto-like hat-pin with which Saxon had been killed. It had been examined by doctors, by finger-print experts, and by Garfield himself— all without result. But it still figured in the investigation. The chief inspector had not consciously reasoned it because the process was so obvious and commonplace to him. Yet if he had, he would have thought in this strain: "Here is a thing which may or may not have been sold in tens of thousands. There is a slim chance that this individual pin may be identified. We will find out where this was manufactured and where in London it has been on retail sale. It is even possible that, through this avenue, we may come upon its ultimate owner."

So a dozen avenues had suggested themselves, some of them branching to blind failure, some with side-alleys, all tending in general by circuitous routes to reach the end of the mystery. Saxon's career, Hilary Sloane, Eston, Saxon's housekeeper, the men at the aeroplane works— all these furnished an infinity of detail work for the searchers. It was one thing to be clear that certain persons were connected with the crime, it was another to find them—and it was still another to gain evidence that would convict. Moral certainties help in detective work, but they do not always convince a jury.

Behind all these trails was Garfield, ready to slip his hounds fully in any direction in which a strong scent should crop up. He had desired grace from Sir Richard Essex before visiting Hilary Sloane's studio in Glebe Crescent, that he might go over his organization and pick up developed during the night. It was little enough, as an outsider might have viewed it, for the amount of energy involved, but the chief inspector was satisfied.

He lit a cigar, slipped on a big coat and with Wade moved along the corridor to intimate to the Assistant-Commissioner his readiness to get along.

"We'll want a search warrant for this place," he explained to Sir Richard. "Might as well be in order you know, sir. Will you sign one?"

"I didn't think of that," confessed the other, who, like all the high administrators of the Metropolitan Police, was an ex officio magistrate —not that he ever sat in court, but to meet such emergencies as these. "I'll see to it."

With the warrant in his pocket, Garfield took his seat in the little brown police car and they slipped away down by the old Abbey towards Chelsea.

VIII

SILVERDALE betook himself for luncheon to the pleasant surroundings of the Palatial Restaurant. Curiously enough, he had scarcely started on his soup when no less a person than Chief Detective-Inspector Garfield dropped heavily into the seat opposite.

Silverdale nodded indifferently. "That you, Garfield? I thought you'd be along. How's everything?"

"Much as usual, Jimmie. What am I going to have?" He studied the menu with deliberate care and chose soundly and solidly.

Jimmie's heart thudded against his ribs. He had steeled himself to this encounter and although outwardly he wore his usual appearance of nonchalant equanimity, he was feeling far from easy. He wondered how much Garfield knew.

Garfield's eyes twinkled. "You've got something up your sleeve just now. I thought we were going to pull this case through together. I just want to know, that's all. What were you doing at Chelsea this morning?"

"So you know about that," said Jimmie slowly. He realized the futility of the remark as he spoke. Of course the police knew all about it. Were not the officers there?

"Yes." The inspector's eyes were still twinkling. It had not yet occurred to him that Jimmie held any personal sentiment in the case. Sooner or later he would know all that Silverdale knew. "You beat us to it by a matter of inches. What have you done with the ladies?"

Silverdale pushed his plate away and brushed back the lock of lank black hair that would persistently fall over his forehead. His eyes looked steadily into those of the detective. "You're all wrong somewhere," he observed with a puzzled note in his voice. "I saw some lady friends of mine off to the seaside this morning. You're not suggesting that they're mixed up in this affair, are you?"

It was not an easy thing to stagger Garfield. He stared helplessly at Silverdale. A thin shadow of suspicion leapt across his mind. Was Silverdale, after all, trying to carry off something by himself? If he had laid his hands on the woman who had killed Harold Saxon and was holding her out of reach of Scotland Yard for some purpose—perhaps to achieve a great scoop for his paper—it would be explicable but for their compact. Silverdale would never go back on an agreement. No, this was somehow just a coincidence, the detective reassured himself.

"You're not trying to fool me, are you?" he asked. "Do you know that one of the women you took away from Glebe Crescent this morning was Hilary Sloane—the girl whom we are looking for? Why—I showed you a photograph."

"You don't mean to tell me—" Jimmie leaned across the table in apparent eagerness—"that you—that Scotland Yard—suspects Miss Sloane! Why, when I saw that picture I put it down as. a mere passing resemblance. Don't be a fool, Garfield. I've known Miss Sloane for—for a long time. I don't suppose she had ever heard of Saxon. It's just mere silliness."

"This is all very damn funny," said Garfield sternly, "but I'm going to get to the bottom of it. I've known coincidences happen but not quite as curious as this. We've been friends a long time, Silverdale, but I strongly advise you to be frank."

"Don't get on your high horse," said Jimmie quietly. "It is a coincidence that you should suspect a friend of mine and I'll give you a piece of advice—don't make a fool of yourself."

Garfield swallowed hard. He had been in danger for a little of losing his temper—a fatal matter in such a situation. "We're getting angry with each other now, Jimmie," he said aud showed his white teeth in a smile.

"Suppose we give up calling each other names and try to straighten this business out. I've never known any person realize at first that a friend could be a criminal. Anyone else's friend, yes, but one's own, never. If you give me your word of honor, Jimmie, that you've never had any suspicion that Hilary Sloane was suspect till this moment, I'll believe you. I'll believe you if you say that it was sheer coincidence that you smuggled her out of Chelsea this morning. But"—his tone changed—"in view of what we found at her studio when we searched it, I'll not believe that she knows nothing of this crime."

"What did you find?"

"We found," said the inspector slowly, "a hatpin, the exact replica of that with which Harold Saxon was murdered."

There was no melodramatic emphasis in the chief inspector's voice. He was merely stating a fact, something as a lawyer presents a fact to a witness in order to Dring out further information. Jimmie, however, apparently remained unmoved. He ate on unperturbed, save for a slight impatient lift of the shoulders.

"Are you trying to manufacture a case against this girl?" he asked coldly. "It looks very much like it to me."

Garfield ignored the charge. To him, coming from a man who knew so much of Scotland Yard methods, it was too absurd to merit resentment.

"Take this hatpin, now," went on Jimmie. "There may be a thousand or ten thousand women wearing that kind of thing."

"There may be," assented the inspector. "Look here, sonny. I'm no Sherlock Holmes and I've seen too many dead certs go wrong ever to be cocksure. What your interest is in this girl I don't know—though I shall know. My business is to add two and two together. I have found it makes five, but not very often. Listen, Jimmie! Here first of all we have Hilary Sloane's picture in possession of the murdered man. Point number one. We know that she was in association with Eston who instigated a

burglary at Saxon's flat for certain papers. Point number
two. She disappears after the murder,(with your help).
Point number three. A hatpin, similar to the one with
which Saxon was murdered, is found in her studio. Point
number four. That may be manufacturing a case in your
view. In mine, I can only say that I'd deserve to be broke
if I didn't follow up that singular string of coincidences. I
don't say she's guilty; only a blind man could maintain
that she is not suspect."

"I gather you suspect her," said Silverdale dryly.

He was doing some hard thinking. He knew, none
better, the bull-dog tenacity with which men like
Garfield, backed by the whole resources of Scotland Yard,
would follow up a trail. The simile of a stoat flashed
across his mind—a stoat comparatively slow but following
a rabbit with deadly methodical unswerving precision.
Superior activity availed the rabbit little. The end was
inevitable. If Hilary Sloane was innocent—and he held
stoutly in his own mind that she was—she could if she
willed prove her innocence. Sooner or later she would be
put to the test. Every day, every hour that she remained
in concealment would add to the black cloud of suspicion
against her.

Perhaps Garfield guessed something of what was
passing in the other's mind. "I think I see how the land
lies," he said smoothly. "I guess this is a pretty hard thing
for you. You've been used to a seat in the stalls and now
you find yourself on the stage among the actors. Suppose
you forget I'm a Scotland Yard man for a bit and just
remember that we've been pals for a good many years."

"And how long would you forget you're a Scotland
Yard man?"

"Just as long as my duty allowed me. You know I've
got nothing personal in this, Silver. I've got a job to do
and I'm going to do it. But I'm not going to hurt anyone
more than I can help. It might be easier for you to trust
me."

The gaze of the two men met—long, steady, and

appraising.

"If I don't?" asked Silverdale.

"It will make no difference. It will be a little longer way round, that's all. We'll get there in the end."

"And if—if you got what you considered proof—if you found that Hilary Sloane—"

Jimmie did not complete the sentence. He was striving to read the other's face. Garfield had finished his lunch and was meditatively chewing a toothpick.

"We haven't got that far yet," he said. "It's always a long way from suspicion to evidence that will convict. That's where the detective of fiction has a pull over us, Jimmie. I've seen detectives—in novels—have a man hanged on evidence that would not convict a dog in real life."

"But if— "persisted the journalist.

"If there was strong evidence pointing to Hilary Sloane," said Garfield sternly, "—something much stronger than there is at present,— I should only have one course to take. She would be arrested and the facts placed before a jury. They would be the judges. If, however, this girl is innocent, you cannot do better than trust me. All I want is the truth."

Silverdale's hands clenched and unclenched beneath the table. He was curiously irresolute. I'll take you at your word, Garfield," he exclaimed in sudden resolve. "Hilary has no guilty knowledge—of that I am convinced. God help me if I'm doing wrong. Listen!"

He had become convinced that the open policy was the best. He talked quickly, tensely, with now and then a sharp nervous gesture to emphasize a point, painting a picture of the girl and her character with all the vivacity and skill of a man practiced in description. Garfield did not interrupt till he had finished, chewing his toothpick stolidly and drumming with his fingers on the tablecloth.

"That is Hilary Sloane," concluded Silverdale. "Is that the sort of woman to commit murder?"

"Murder is not crime in the ordinary sense,"

commented the detective. "A person may be honest, courageous, straightforward, even lovable, and still be a murderer—or murderess." He spoke the last words as an afterthought. "In spite of all you have told me, you know little of this girl. You don't even know her antecedents before you met her."

"I don't need to. I know Miss Sloane and that is enough. Do you know anything against her?" The words were a challenge.

"No—but I shall," said Garfield. "I hope it will clear things up. Now the thing is for you to get me in touch with her."

"That's impossible," said Jimmie.

"Impossible—why?"

"Because she has disappeared. I had a wire from my aunt before I left the office. Miss Sloane and Miss Dring should have reached her before ten o'clock. They had not got there by eleven."

"H'm?" The detective put an interrogation note into his interjection.

"I'm hoping it may be all right. They may have been delayed—missed their connection at Reading—there may be some very simple explanation." He had risen and was struggling into his overcoat. A waiter came forward to assist him and he checked himself till he had settled the bill and the functionary had gone. "But I've got an uneasy feeling—and if anything has happened I may want your help."

"H'm," commented the inspector again. "Sure you're not being played with, Jimmie? Now, suppose this lady— it's only supposition, mind—is not the angel you think her. It might suit her book not to arrive. She might want to dodge like a hare."

"I'd pledge my immortal soul she'd play the game with me," asserted Jimmie. "There's something gone wrong if she isn't there. What's this Eston man got to do with her, anyway? I didn't tell you that I met him an hour or two ago—immediately after I'd seen the girls off."

He repeated the story of his encounter outside Paddington Station as they walked out. Garfield's face changed as he listened. He smacked Silverdale on the back and laughed softly.

"Jimmie, if you wanted to convert me to your point of view about Hilary Sloane, why didn't you tell me this first? I'll suspend opinion on her."

"But you have always known that Eston was in the case somewhere."

"Sure I did. But I didn't know he was so vitally interested that he'd do such a senseless thing as that. He's a cold, callous rogue,"— Garfield used another word,—"and if he wasn't deep in this, he'd not take the risk of interfering now. He'd not lift a finger for Miss Sloane, yet he wants to head us off. There's a deep game on here, Jimmie, and I'm hanged if I see the bottom of it. Could he have intercepted the girls after he left you?"

Silverdale shook his head. "Not if the train was on time."

"Well, this makes it more or less essential that I see Miss Sloane and get her story. You will see to that, Jimmie?"

"Come back to the office with me now and we'll see if there are any wires."

The inspector glanced at his watch. "I'm with you," he said shortly, and held up his hand for a taxi.

It was typical of Garfield that he would not accompany Silverdale inside when they reached the *Daily Wire* offices. He preferred to sit remotely back in the recesses of the car and wait. Presently Silverdale returned, two wires in his hand. He looked very serious.

"They have not arrived," he said.

"Ah!"

"What do you make of this? It's from my aunt." He handed over one of the wires and Garfield read:

"Girls not arrived just got telegram tell jimmie twyford don't understand."

The British telegraph system is a wonderful

institution but it has some defects. Its neglect of
punctuation is apt to throw some messages into
incoherence. The detective wrestled with it for a second
and read it aloud, putting in the proper pauses.

"Girls not arrived. Just got telegram: 'Tell Jimmie
Twyford.' Don't understand."

"I don't like it," he said portentously. "Somehow or
other the girls have been lured off the train at Twyford—
a riverside station on the Great Western line, a few miles
this side of Reading." He thrust his head through the
window. "Hi! driver! New Scotland Yard."

"Why lured off? They may have stopped off at their
own free will."

"Scarcely, in the circumstances. If Miss Sloane sent
that wire she sent it in a hurry or she would have been
more explicit. She wants you to know where she is. She
had only time to write the address and three words. It
suggests she was under compulsion."

"Eston?"

"Maybe. There's a frame-up here and I think I see his
hand."

Silverdale rolled a cigarette. "I'll drop you at the
Yard," he said. "I'm going to Twyford."

"Call it ten minutes at the Yard, Jimmie, and I'll come
with yon. I want to see this girl and it won't do any harm,
if things are as I think, that you should have company."

As a matter of fact, Garfield took less than ten
minutes. He left a man at the telephone, putting through
a call, to the police at Twyford, had a brief interview with
Superintendent Winter, grabbed a budget of papers from
his desk, which he stuck in his pocket, and was leaving
when he came face to face with Wade.

"We've got on to Velvet," said the sergeant.

"That's good. Grab him and keep him till I get back
this evening. I've got to get down to Twyford."

"That's funny," said Wade. "Velvet left for Reading on
an early morning train. I am getting in touch with the
Reading police."

Garfield placed a hand on his shoulder and twisted him round. "You'll do no such thing," he declared. "You'll come along with me down to Twyford. We'll get Velvet there if we want him. And, Wade—I nearly forgot—you might slip up and get me three automatic pistols if you don't mind. I don't like the beastly things, but they're useful to have on occasion."

IX

HILARY SLOANE was by nature an extravagant and luxurious little person. She could rough it uncomplainingly on occasion, but when opportunity offered she preferred to be comfortable. So it was that, aided and abetted by Nora Dring, she invested in first-class tickets after they left Jimmie Silverdale—lavishness all the more fascinating because they could not really afford them.

They found that they had, after all, ample time to settle themselves comfortably before the train started. Nora bought two or three illustrated papers and fumbled with them as she maintained a conversation that both at first strove to keep as commonplace as though they were merely leaving London on a holiday. Nora Dring was, however, in spite of many masculine qualities, a woman. The repression of curiosity was hateful to her.

"I rather like your Mr. Silverdale," she observed.

"He has been very good to us," agreed Hilary. Nora leaned back with feline grace. She had the pussy-cat habit of physical comfort. From under her long, silky eyelashes she regarded her companion steadily.

"What were you talking about before I came down this morning?"

Hilary turned over the pages of the magazine in her lap. "Oh, things," she retorted vaguely.

Outside a whistle blew and the train began to draw out from the station. Nora drew a morocco case from her hand bag, selected a delicately scented cigarette and, with a graceful gesture of her slim, white hand, applied a light. She gave a few tentative puffs and gazed after the smoke rings as they disappeared to the roof.

"He must have thought everything very mysterious,"

she commented.

Hilary folded her magazine and laid it on the seat beside her. She began to appreciate the drift of Nora's questioning and whither it might lead. Nora Dring had been her friend for a long time, but she had come to realize in this last day or two that people may be intimately associated with each other for long periods without in the least understanding each other's personality.

"He probably did," she fenced.

"I'm wondering what he knew—what he asked you," went on Nora. "It wasn't like you to fall into a faint." She blew on the red end of her cigarette and watched the ash flutter away. Then her eyes turned to her friend.

Hilary flushed, but met the gaze of the other girl squarely. "I flatter myself I worked that stunt rather well," she said flippantly. "Do you know, Nora, all this kind of thing reminds me of a picture-palace drama. I just carried out the atmosphere. It was the right thing for the distressed heroine to faint at that moment. Some little actress—what!"

Two thin, hard lines appeared between Nora's brows. "That's all nonsense," she said brusquely. "This superficial cynicism does not impose on me. I want to hear how much Jimmie Silverdale knows. Don't play with me, Hilary. Let's have this out. I'm not a child and I'm not going to be led blindfold any longer." She threw her cigarette away and ground her heel on it viciously. Her lips were set resolutely and there was more than a suggestion in her voice of a schoolmistress lecturing a stubborn child.

"Don't be silly," Hilary laughed, but there was resentment in her gray eyes. "You agreed to leave matters to me. Let me manage this."

Nora shifted to the seat beside her and caught her hand. "Forgive me, Hilary, but I must know." Her voice had lost its menacing accent and was coaxing, persuasive. "Do you remember when we were a pair of silly little

flappers together that we swore we'd never have secrets
from one another as long as we lived?"

"Did we? I suppose we've carried out that compact—
more or less!" There was no missing the irony in Hilary's
voice. "You have had no secrets from me all this time. I
can make allowances, Nora, but you are putting a strain
on my loyalty to you." She flung out a hand impulsively.
"Aren't there any questions I should like to ask you—
questions burning in my brain even now. I want to know
"she checked herself.

Nora withdrew, white-lipped. "What?" she demanded.

"Oh, nothing. Let's drop the subject."

"I will not. I'm going to thrash this thing out. You
have been talking to Mr. Silverdale. He has questioned
you. He knows something. I know this, Hilary—you are in
love with him. You appealed to him for help, and he is
using you for some purpose. You are just a silly little
fool!"

Hilary stiffened a little and took the seat that Nora
had vacated a few minutes before so that they were again
face to face. Her Red Cross training warned her that her
friend was rapidly developing all the symptoms of a form
of hysteria. She had fought long with her own high spirit
to restrain herself, but now the limit had been
overstepped. Two spots of high, red color appeared in her
cheeks.

"Then I'll tell you," she said coldly.

Nora leaned forward, her elbows on her knee, her chin
between her cupped bands, and her eyes fixed tensely on
her friend.

"Mr. Silverdale," went on Hilary, articulating the
words with vivid distinctness, "asked me what I knew of
the murder of Sir Harold Saxon. It was then I fainted."

A cold shiver shook Nora Dring from head to foot. Her
face had gone ashen and she put a hand out blindly.
Something like a moan escaped her lips.

"He accused you of the murder?"

"He warned me I was suspected," said Hilary stonily.

"And yet—and yet he helped you—us—to get away."
Nora shook herself as though to be freed from some
physical affliction. "It's a trap, Hilary. He is playing with
you." She fell on her knees, sobbing, and buried her face
in Hilary's lap.

A score of questions were on Hilary's lips—questions
suppressed for long, but the answers to which would have
supplied the key to a riddle that was torturing her. She
bit them back and her hand fell gently on Nora's head.
Very gently she fondled the distraught girl, murmuring
little endearments that one would use to a sobbing child.

Presently Nora rose abruptly to her feet. She had
become extraordinarily calm. Her face was as impassive
as though carved in stone. A complete mastery of herself
had returned to her.

"It is a trap," she repeated earnestly. "He is hand in
glove with the police. He is putting us where they can lay
their hands on us when they have completed their
evidence."

"I trust Mr. Silverdale," said Hilary simply. "We can
separate, if you like." Yet a cold hand seemed to grip at
her heart. Silverdale had told her that the detectives
were linking up evidence that might implicate her. She
was a woman of cool common-sense, though her apparent
jaunty indifference to consequences had sometimes
deluded observers. She could estimate a situation as well
as most men and she realized where she stood. But she
hated herself for suggesting that she should draw out.
Nora made no answer. She thrust her head through the
window and Hilary remembered later, although she was
not conscious of deliberately observing it, that she seemed
to make some gesture. Then she commenced to sort out
her traveling impedimenta and the train drew up at a
station. Hilary caught a glimpse of the name Twyford on
a signboard, and then a figure darkened the window.

"Good-morning, Miss Dring. Good-morning, Miss
Sloane. None the worse for your very hurried journey, I
hope?"

Eston, hat in hand, and a dark mark on his face was opening the door, suave and smiling and sinister. Hilary shrank back in her seat.

"You?"

"Yes, even so humble a person as myself, Miss Sloane. I was traveling by this train, though I caught it by so narrow a margin that I had no time to seek the privilege of traveling in such pleasant company. I was a little delayed by an interview with a friend of yours, Miss Sloane—a Mr. Silverdale. Can I assist you to get your things out?"

"Thank you," said Hilary icily. "I'm going on."

A quick glance passed between Nora Dring and Eston—a glance that seemed to carry a question and answer. Nora was no longer the sobbing, distraught being of a few minutes before. Instead she was calm and business-like as she hurriedly passed the luggage out.

"I think you had better get out here, Hilary."

"I refuse. Nora, you'll be mad to trust this man. If you go with him, I wash my hands of the whole business."

Eston laughed. "I'm afraid your opinion of me has changed, Miss Sloane. Let me assure you,"—there was menace in his tone—"that yon are going to get out here. You are too valuable to us to be allowed to go astray. You know too much—much that might be interesting to Mr. Silverdale, or the police. I propose to keep a fatherly eye on you. Now I'd hate to use force but—"

Hilary remained unmoved, though her nerves were tense. Whatever her relations with Eston had been, there could now be no doubt that she thoroughly distrusted him.

"I have heard a great deal about you since we last met, Mr. Eston," she said. "If you lay a finger on me, believe me, I shall not be afraid to create a scene!"

He still wore the suave, unpleasant smile. "You will come quietly," he insisted. "Otherwise it will be embarrassing for me to explain to the station-master that you are a lady mentally afflicted, traveling in charge of

Miss Dring here. Ask yourself if the officials are likely to believe any wild tale you tell."

There was no doubt in Hilary's mind that he was bluffing and all her inclinations were to let him attempt to carry it out to the end. It was inconceivable that so barefaced an attempt at abduction could be successfully carried out in broad daylight at a railway station. But then there was another point to be considered. If the threat to force her were put into execution— and now she knew that Nora would undoubtedly side with him—it would mean something more than a rather unpleasant interlude. It would attract to them an attention that she did not desire at that moment. She was in a sense a fugitive. It might lead to anything—even to a police call as a murder suspect. Better far to appear to submit until some better opportunity arose for deciding a course of action.

She rose with a shrug of her shoulders, "I am buying experience," she said. "I'll submit. But I warn you that, after this, I hold myself free to act as I choose. Now I gave you my word of honor on certain matters. This absolves me."

Nora Dring did not meet her eyes. "I'm sorry, Hilary," she said. "Believe me, we're acting for the best. It is your interest, as well as ours."

"You're just a pawn in this game," interposed Eston, "and pawns have to be sacrificed sometimes."

The train glided out as soon as she had alighted. Eston hurried in search of a porter to see to the luggage and Nora busied herself, woman-fashion, in piling it into a nearer heap. Hilary extracted an envelope from her hand bag and hurriedly scrawled the wire that Silverdale was to receive some hours later. As Eston and a porter arrived, she, like Nora, fussed with the luggage, adjusting it on the hand-barrow, awaiting her opportunity. Presently she thrust the message and a ten-shilling note into the man's hand.

"Send that for me," she said quietly. "Don't let my

friends know."

The porter nodded. "Right-oh, miss. I understand. I'll see that it goes off."

Outside the station, a fly of the antiquated kind that can only be found in the pleasure resorts of England was waiting. Eston had, apparently, already given instructions to the driver, for the moment they had taken their seats, he drove off at a steady jog trot.

Hilary smoothed her skirt. "Nora," she said, "since you seem to have arranged all this, perhaps you can tell me what it means. Am I a prisoner?"

"A prisoner!" interposed Eston. 'I hope you won't get that idea, Miss Sloane. Shall we not say a guest—an honored guest!"

X

GARFIELD and Jimmie were busy. It was easy enough to pick up the trail at the Twyford station. It was simplicity itself to find the driver of the fly who had taken Eston and the two girls to some unknown destination. But there they stuck.

"I was told to drive them out three miles on the Reading road," explained the cab-driver. "They tumbled out on a lonely piece of highway and there I left them— luggage and all."

"Wasn't there a house near?" asked Garfield.

"Not so much as a hut on either side for near three quarters of a mile. The gent was a pleasant-mannered man. He gave me a brown Bradbury."

"He gave you a pound," said Silverdale. "How did things strike you? Were they all friendly and happy together?"

The cab-driver jerked his head in assent. Everything was quite all right. People did odd things at times, he pointed out, emphasizing the observation with the stem of his pipe, and for his part he was content to mind his own business whatever kind of place people got down at. Yes, he'd very willingly drive the gentlemen out the same way to the same spot. Might he be so bold as to inquire whether it was a runaway match? He was a man as minded his own business, but he always kept his eyes and ears open, he did. As soon as he set eyes on the party, he knew there was going to be an elopement. Which one of the young ladies was it, might he ask? A pretty-looking pair, but girls weren't what they were in his young days. He ventured to suppose that—looking hard at Garfield— his girl had, so to speak, got the bit between her teeth.

The chief inspector came as near to a blush as his constitution would permit and cut the old man's garrulity short. "I'm no relation to either of these ladies," he observed testily. "Suppose you get us along now. Wade— just a second." He drew his subordinate aside and gave some instructions in a low voice. Wade nodded understandingly and faded away. He had a habit of fading unobtrusively for, though, like all Scotland Yard folk he was a big man, he could be very inconspicuous when he chose.

Neither Silverdale nor Garfield attached much hope of learning anything from their expedition out of Twyford. It was just one of those episodes which are continually cropping up in investigation work where the guiding axiom is not to neglect anything. They were able to make a shrewd guess as to what had happened.

"I suppose dear old Sherlock Holmes would learn something from this," said Garfield when they had arrived, surveying the grassy bank, where the fugitive party had been set down, with furrowed brow. "It doesn't need any genius to gather that Eston wouldn't come here on the spur of the moment. He had some fixed plan in his mind and he was taking no chances oi making an easy track for us to follow — if we got on this end at all. They 've been picked up here by motor-car, and lord only knows where they've been spirited off to."

A little two-seated motor-car that was approaching slid to a standstill near them, and one of the occupants alighted. He looked something like a robust farmer.

"Am I speaking to Chief-Detective Inspector Garfield?" he asked.

"That's me."

"Ah, yes. My name is Grimes. I am superintendent of this division of the county constabulary. I heard you had arrived and followed your cab out here. It's the Saxon business, I suppose. I know you are on it. "

"Pleased to meet you, Mr. Grimes. Shake with my friend, Mr. Silverdale. Yes, we thought we might run an end down this way, but nothing seems likely to come of it."

Grimes took out a well-worn brier pipe and pressed down the tobacco in the bowl with a thick thumb. "I don't know so much about that, Mr. Garfield. We're not all fools in the provincial police forces, though some of your people up at Scotland Yard seem to think so."

"Some people do run away with the idea that Scotland Yard is the big noise," assented Garfield genially. "I've never believed it myself. The Yard gets more chances, that's all. I was going to call on you, but decided to wait until I'd been out here."

Silverdale turned away to hide a smile. Officially the various police forces of the United Kingdom work in complete accord and harmony together. Actually things are not always harmonious. Time and again he had heard London men consign their provincial colleagues to the nether regions as arrant fools; no less often provincial officers had expressed their private but emphatic view that Scotland Yard was a school for stuck-up blighting idiots.

"Pity you didn't," said Grimes. "Might have saved you a lot of trouble. We got a message this morning asking us to watch for three people who had reached Twyford by an early train—two women and a man. Their descriptions came along, too, so I had some inquiries made and a look-out kept."

"They drove out as far as this spot and then changed into a motor-car?"

"You're right, Mr. Garfield. That car was hired in Reading and came out to meet them here. They've flitted back to London, so you've had a wasted journey." He blew a cloud of smoke into the air. "Which of them in particular is the bird you're after?"

Garfield shot a quick glance at his interlocutor and a puzzled look crept into his face. "All of 'em," he said briefly. "I guess I've met you before, haven't I, Mr. Grimes? There's something about you I seem to remember, though I can't seem to place you. I haven't been down this way officially before."

"I think I ran across you some time ago when I was nosing around the Criminal Record Office. I was an inspector there—but you probably wouldn't remember me."

"It may be so," agreed Garfield indifferently, strolling a few paces forward so that Grimes was between Silverdale and himself.

"I'd like to know a little more about this business if you'll trust me."

The detective-inspector thrust his face forward until it was within a few inches of Grimes. His jaw jutted out and his eyes were stern. But his voice was mild.

"Sure about that, old man?" he asked. "Sure?"

"What the blazes—" Grimes took a step or two backwards, but Garfield followed him up, pace for pace.

"I'm thinking that you know too much about this already," he declared. "That little party has not gone to London. It's here—or some of it. You've got a nerve, Eston, but we've got you cold this time. You've overstepped things for once."

He leapt as he spoke and the other man by a quick movement tried to evade his grip. But Garfield was an adept in this kind of thing and his powerful hands had fastened around Eston's waist in less time than the flicker of an eyelid might have taken.

Jimmie's first impulse was to fling himself headlong into the scrap, but he checked himself. Garfield he believed to be fully capable of dealing with Eston in a physical tussle. It was a more vital matter to see that Eston's companion, the driver of the two-seater, did not intervene. Silverdale turned towards the car.

"You keep there!" he warned.

The driver had his eyes fixed on the twisting, struggling men and scarcely lifted them to the journalist. "That's all right, guv'nor. Don't you worry about me. I'm not rushing to mix myself up in that, believe me."

"Better not," advised Jimmie, and threw a quick glance on the struggling pair, while standing so that he might intervene if the chauffeur should change his mind. There could be no comparison physically between the struggling pair. Garfield in weight, height, and strength hopelessly outmatched his opponent. Eston, however, was fighting desperately. The hat and wig that had formed part of his make-up for the character of Grimes had fallen to the ground and oily beads of perspiration were rolling down his forehead and cheeks. Garfield clasped him round the body and was letting him exhaust himself in fruitless struggles. His head was tucked down, boring into Eston's face to avoid the blows the other was trying to shower on him. The two twisted round and round slowly as though in a strange eccentric dance, for Eston's feet—now heavily shod in support of the character he was impersonating—were making their mark on the detective's legs.

"'Olds him like a grizzly bear," commented the driver with the casual tone of a detached observer. "'E'll crush 'im to death if 'e's not careful."

Indeed, the futility of the fight seemed to have occurred to Eston for he fell limp all of a sudden and became a dead weight in Garfield's arms.

"I'm all in," he muttered. "Let me go." Garfield was breathing a little faster than usual. He relaxed the pressure but maintained his hold. "Not on your life," he observed with decision. "You're too slippery a customer to monkey with. Jimmie, come over here. I want to borrow your handkerchief."

It is one of the scandals of our time that Scotland Yard men do not always carry themselves in a manner befitting popular expectation. The Public believes that every criminal hunter carries a pair of handcuffs on his person, ready to snap instantly on the wrists of any wrong-doer. As a matter of fact, handcuffs are only carried by men on escort duty. Garfield, like his colleagues, would in the ordinary course of duty be as likely to find a use for a Lewis gun as for handcuffs.

The detective with a quick movement shifted his grip

to Eston's arms and forced them behind his back. The other made no resistance.

"You're making a mistake, Garfield," he observed in a quiet voice. "You've got no evidence of an offense against me."

"Jimmie," said Garfield, "just knot your handkerchief about this gentleman's wrists."

He shifted his position on the grass and the prisoner conformed to his movements, but the movement afforded Eston the chance for which he was looking. His leg twined round the detective who was caught at a precarious balance and tumbled backwards into a ditch, releasing Eston in a wild effort to save himself. Almost at the same time the car began to move as the watchful driver, no longer so impassive as when Jimmie's eyes had been on him, thrust in the clutch.

Luck was with Eston. As Jimmie grabbed at him, he swerved and the slippery grass for which the reporter had made no allowances did the rest. Jimmie sat down keavily. Before either he or Garfield had regained their feet, the little two-seater was twenty yards up the road and gathering speed.

It is in such contingencies, that a sense of humor is a great asset. Jimmie looked at Garfield, and Garfield looked at Jimmie. The detective was rueful, but there was a twinkle in his eye. They burst into laughter—laughter at their own chagrin. If they had not laughed, they would have cursed.

The ancient fly-driver, who had sat throughout a detached and open-mouthed observer of the affair, thought they were mad.

XI

GARFIELD it was who suggested that they should walk back to the station and, having paid off the "hearse," they started on their tramp. For ten minutes or so, the inspector marched in silence. Then he glanced whimsically at Jimmie.

"Got it worked out?" he asked.

Silverdale shook his head. "You've got more of the thread in your hand than I have. I'd hate to make a guess. I'll admit that I never had a doubt that Grimes was Grimes until you sprang it that he was Eston. That was a beautiful bit of camouflage."

"Its very audacity disarmed you, Jimmie. There's no doubt that I'd have fallen for it, too, but that I was worried by something—it may have been the voice or the manner, or the appearance, or the man's anxiety to know things. I don't know how many hundreds of inspectors of provincial police there are in this country, and I give my word, I couldn't keep tab of 'em, even if I knew 'em. However, when he introduced himself, I had a vague idea that I'd heard or seen the name somewhere before and that, with my uneasiness, set my memory hard at work. There wasn't any Sherlocking or identification business required. I remembered a little two-line paragraph that I'd seen a fortnight ago, telling of the presentation of a gold watch to Superintendent Grimes on *his retirement.* Eston fell because of that little point. I don't pretend I'd have known him until I began to look for someone, other than a police officer."

"Yes, but why should he do it? This is the second time. He pulled me up in town, when I shouldn't have known him from Adam. Why go out of his way to look for us? I'd have thought he'd have bolted down his burrow and let us do all the worrying in this game of touch."

The inspector slipped his arm through Silverdale's.

"So would I, if he were not Eston. I can think of fifty reasons for his action, but I'm not sure which is the right one. That's why I let him go just now."

It has been said before that Chief-Detective Inspector Garfield had a certain amount of human nature in his composition. He was an able man and though he scorned the appreciation of mediocrities, like all able men, he was not averse from a certain nai'veness in displaying his cleverness in a quiet way. From the corner of his eyes he watched Silverdale's face for a due expression of surprise before he sprang any further information. Jimmie Silverdale, however, showed no surprise. He gave a tiny jerk of the head and flung a cigarette butt into the hedge.

"So you had a reason—or fifty reasons. I thought something of that kind was in your mind. I'm glad I was right. It would have hurt me to think that he got away if you really wanted him."

"You—you—" Garfield choked. "Why, you scoundrel, you don't mean to say you did the same thing? You let him go, also?"

"I took a chance. It seemed to me that, for a man of your experience, that slip was too easy. You'd decided to let Eston go and it wasn't for me to butt in and spoil whatever you'd got in your mind. So I did a bit of play-acting myself. Otherwise it wouldn't have been convincing. "

"Well, I'm not quite sure whether we've done right or wrong. Eston is likely to be a handful, but if I'd taken him then, he might have slipped through our fingers with the help of a shrewd lawyer. You see, legally, there is nothing against him so far as the murder is concerned. Actually, of course, if he didn't kill Saxon, he is bound up in the business. I want to know where. He's taking big risks in a big way and that means something. He may give us the slip but on the whole the odds are that if we do get anything definite to act on we'll be able to find him. He's playing a game. Our last chance of finding out what that game is, is, as a respected politician put it, to 'wait and see.'"

"You think—" Silverdale hesitated—"have you still the idea that Hilary Sloane is concerned with it?"

"I reserve judgment. She is fitted into Eston's scheme somehow, whether as pawn or something bigger it is hard to say. I'm as anxious as ever to see that young lady, Jimmie, and I'll admit that is one reason why I played bogey just now. Here's a point. She and Miss Dring are in this neighborhood somewhere, for Eston wouldn't have hung about merely for play-acting with us. Velvet Fred left for Reading this morning—there's no reason why he shouldn't have dropped off here. Everything points the same way."

"Then Hilary—Miss Sloane—"

"If it's any relief to you, I'll own one thing. It looks to me more probable that Miss Sloane is innocent than that she is guilty. This wire she sent you rather gives one the impression that she has become unwilling to help out Eston and his gang, whatever her associations with them were before. She's had some strong motive for her actions all through—if I could get her, I'd have a lead through this tangle."

Garfield was careful to leave himself a loophole. Hilary Sloane might still be guilty, though he had his own reasons for thinking she might not. Jimmie was not slow to grasp the impression that had formed in the inspector's mind.

"I'd stake my immortal soul on her innocence, " lie said earnestly.

"I've heard you say something like that before, " commented Garfield dryly. "Personally, I wouldn't stake a new hat on anyone's innocence in a matter of murder. I have found many murderers very nice people, Jimmie. They have to be hanged, as a rule, and that is why I oppose indiscriminate capital punishment. The psychology of murder is a very deep subject and I've looked for the truth in a number of high-brow books on criminology and never found it. Now over a good many years I've come to a conclusion that is clean against all the detective writers. They assume—it's part of their trade, I suppose—that the obvious solution to a crime problem is invariably the wrong one. My own view is that, in nine cases out of ten, it's right.

"Now Hilary Sloane is a woman and when women commit crimes of violence, as a general rule they don't calculate too much on their chances of making a getaway. In calculated crimes by women, they use poison rather than the knife or pistol. If crime could be reduced to absolute principles that would let women out on all these affairs. There are, however, a hundred different factors in these cases and the probability of a woman being concerned cannot be dismissed. Getting down to this concrete case, there is the fact that some physical force was necessary to tie Saxon up. There was premeditation all through and though a woman's hatpin was used, in my view the chances are that it was not a woman."

A springiness had come into Jimmie's step as the detective talked. A heavy weight had been taken from his mind and he broke out into a cheerful whistle. The chief inspector smiled quietly at the hedge-row. Then Jimmie's whistle broke off abruptly.

"On your theory—"

"I don't hold theories," interrupted Garfield. "They're too dangerous for the Criminal Investigation Department."

"On your supposition, then, Miss Sloane is being held a prisoner by Eston against her will?"

"Something of that sort. I'm not sure it's against her will. Eston has some hold on her."

"Ah." The journalist became thoughtful. "What's the next move? How do you propose to smoke them out?"

Garfield paused to light his pipe. Then he stooped to brush his trousers with a handkerchief. "Can't keep clean in the country," he grumbled. "Well, to tell you the truth,

Jimmie, I propose to go through this country with a fine-tooth comb. You can't hide three able-bodied people in these days. It's a sheer impossibility. And just for once I'm going to look to you to give a hand while I use my own methods. It's up to you to become a publicity agent. With the help of the *Daily Wire*, we ought to get 'em."

Jimmie shook his head resolutely. "No good, Garfield. I hate to refuse but I'm not going to drag Miss Sloane's name through, the mud and slops of a murder case."

"Don't lose your sense of perspective, old lad," said Garfield. "I don't want to alarm you, but you must remember that this lady is in Eston's power." He brought down a heavy fist into the palm of an open hand. "We've simply got to find her. You may regret it all your life if you neglect a single chance. Don't use her name unless you like. But give her description, her photograph, everything that you can to arouse public interest. You can tell the whole story—with discretion, of course —but, for Heaven's sake, get on to it, Jimmie. You must!"

The journalist smoked furiously while he considered the proposition. He hated the idea of smudging Hilary Sloane's name by turning on her the great searchlight of the Press. It is not a nice thing to be associated with a *cause celebre*, however innocent one may be. Nor, in the light of his knowledge of Garfield, was he altogether inclined to be too trusting.

Yet, on the other hand, if the case ever reached a criminal court, Hilary would obviously be a witness. She could not be kept out of the picture in the ultimate result. To hold his hand would merely delay matters. Again, the girl was in Eston's power. If the great weapon he had at his disposal could ensure that the business would be over a week—even a day —or an hour sooner—was it not his business to use it? In any case he could not prevent Garfield from doing so. There were other papers than the *Daily Wire*—other reporters than Jimmie Silverdale.

"Garfield," he said soberly, "you've gathered that I hope to persuade Miss Sloane to marry me some day."

The inspector nodded. "I appreciate that, Jimmie. If for that reason alone you should do as I say. If I told you Eston's reputation"

Jimmie slipped a finger round the inside of the tall collar he affected. "Yes—I'll do it," he said slowly. "I don't know whether I'm right or not, but I'll do it."

XII

IT is possible that the public does not always appreciate the fact that a paper has scored over its rivals in the matter of news so keenly as newspaperland itself. A "scoop" is often rather a moral than a material triumph; but nevertheless it is an ambition keen as a razor edge with every editorial man on a daily paper. Yet for purposes of his own Silverdale had committed the deadly newspaper sin. He had deliberately and with his eyes open sacrificed the scoop he held regarding the disappearance of Hilary Sloane. It was a lapse which, if known to the mandarins of the *Daily Wire*, would have caused an epidemic of apoplexy.

For the time, however, Jimmie's professional ethics had been swamped. If publicity was to be used in finding Hilary Sloane he was determined to use it to the nth degree if necessary. So it was that four papers chronicled what some of them were pleased to call the new and startling development of the Saxon murder story. It was the ancient hue and cry applied by modern methods. Tens of thousands of people suddenly found themselves discussing with intimate interest the search for the two girls and Eston. The public, as the news-editor of the *Daily Wire* prophesied, simply ate it.

Certain details, of course, were never published at all. Jimmie was discreet. It was easy to show Hilary simply as an innocent victim of circumstance. Nor did he absolutely let his own paper down. His personal narrative of Garfield's encounter with Eston was some salve to the *Daily Wire* for the escape of the main story into the columns of its rivals.

No longer was it merely the organization of Scotland Yard against Eston—the whole population of the country

was, so to speak, called in to aid in the search. Yet this
wholesale method of investigation had its disadvantages.
While the newspapermen and the detectives concentrated
on the district round about Twyford in an effort to pick up
the scent, there began an avalanche of false trails.

Some had seen Hilary at Forest Hill, Newcastle,
Glasgow, Bristol, and Cornwall. Here she was alone,
there she was accompanied by Eston and Miss Dring.
There was scarce a district in the country where she had
not been seen. Some of the informants were hazy and
general; others were definite and circumstantial. All were
seeking to aid justice, though a few hinted that some
more substantial recognition should be theirs. A little
sifting reduced the majority of the stories that passed into
Scotland Yard and the newspaper offices to their true
proportions, but the rest caused more trouble. It is never
safe in such cases to ignore anything nor to assume
offhand that the unlikely is unnecessarily untrue.

On the other hand, much was learnt about Eston and
the two girls that would have taken weeks to gather in
the ordinary way. In consequence, both Garfield and
Silverdale were much engaged in office work during the
day, leaving the hunt at Twyford to others for the time
being. It was late in the afternoon that the two met at
Paddington. The chief inspector was rubbing his hands
gleefully.

"We're beginning to move, Silver," he said. "I'd hate to
brag but we're likely to get to the bottom of this show
much quicker than I expected."

"Can you lay your hands on Eston?" asked Jimmie.

Garfield shook his head and held open the door of a
compartment for his companion. "All that in good time,"
he said as he took his own seat. "That's the thing we'll
deal with next. I've been more concerned to disentangle
the evidence. It's been office work all day for me. Have
you got anything fresh?"

"Several odds and ends—I've sent everything that
seemed important up to the Yard."

"Ah!" Garfield leaned back and stretched his arms above his head as the train started. "That's what I've been doing—juggling with odds and ends. Would it surprise you, Jimmie, to learn that by no reasonable possibility could Miss Sloane have committed this murder?"

"Is that your idea of humor?" queried Silverdale icily. "I could have told you that."

"In fact you did," agreed the inspector amiably. "Don't fly off the handle, Jimmie. I want to talk to you. I feel like Sherlock Holmes and I need a Watson."

"Fire ahead."

Garfield rammed his pipe full with tobacco, applied a light and took one or two tentative puffs. "Sir Harold Saxon," he said, "was married in the year before the war. He was just plain Harold Saxon then and was employed as a kind of foreman carpenter at some works in Columbus, Ohio, U. S. A. He was married to an English girl."

"That stuff came from our New York men this morning."

"Precisely. It also came to us from Pinkerton's, from the Mulberry Street detective bureau, and from other sources. I judge your man didn't tell you the name of the lady?"

"No." Silverdale detected something curious in the other's tone.

"The girl he married," went on the other, "gave her name as Hilary Sloane."

"That's a lie." Silverdale spoke quietly, without emphasis, as though he had no personal feeling at all. Garfield regarded him impassively with a twinkle in his eye. Jimmie noted that twinkle and it killed the dread that was arising in his mind.

"It is not a lie. It's the bald truth. What's more, it's plausible. The only thing against it is that Miss Sloane has never been in America. We've carried her record back to her school days and we know for a certainty. Can you begin to put two and two together, Jimmie?"

The journalist leaned forward. It was easy to see that his mind was working fast. "If Hilary was not in America and Saxon married a Hilary Sloane, she may have had a namesake—"

"I thought of that. It's straining coincidence pretty far," commented the other dryly.

"It's so wild that it must be out of the question. Therefore someone must have assumed Hilary Sloane's name—someone who knew her and who wished to be married in an assumed name. Probably the girl had no definite reason for taking that name, rather than any other. Suppose it's—by Heaven, Garfield!"

Garfield's eyes were still twinkling. "I'm supposing nothing off-hand because I hope to know as soon as the mail can carry a photograph. No use in drawing inferences when one can establish facts. We'll keep our guesses on the identity of the lady out of it. Now I'm going to switch to another interesting point. Saxon was being blackmailed."

"That doesn't altogether surprise me. In fact, some of the information we've received about him at the office would show that he'd given opportunities before the war."

"He wasn't worth powder and shot from a blackmailer's point of view before he'd got money," agreed Garfield. "Now we're getting close up to it. His bank account shows gaps that no reasonable explanation but blackmail will cover."

"Surely he never paid by check?"

"Not on your life. I never knew a blackmailer who liked checks. No, Saxon was in some ways a very methodical man. He kept a private account book in which he indicated his own expenditure. Now, over the last six or eight months he drew no less than £3,700—quite apart from his own personal expenditure which he showed clearly—in sums ranging from £1,000 to £400. Contrary to his usual habits, he presented a check himself and drew it in small notes. Now that is quite a sum and small notes are hard to trace. The last payment was made six months ago.

"That," went on Garfield, "narrows things down. It may have been his wife; it may have been someone else. I suspect that Eston has had a hand in it. It is quite likely that he had to know that Saxon had married someone who called herself Hilary Sloane. Whether he knew or not that she was Saxon's real wife is a point one cannot be certain of. If he believed she was actually Lady Saxon, it would explain much of his methods at the moment—for the real Lady Saxon will hold a large interest in the fortune that the dead man has left. Eston always plays for big stakes.

"Now here is a hypothesis which may be right or wrong, but which gives us a working assumption for the moment. Suppose Eston was the blackmailer and suppose Saxon had at last got tired of being bled and made a stand. Eston might very well decide to play the big game—even though it meant murder. He might see his way to get the girl he believed to be Saxon's wife under his control—*and with Saxon's fortune.* Do you follow?"

Jimmie made a gesture of assent. "I can see holes in your reasoning, but I believe you're on the line. That would explain why Eston was so anxious to enlist me—if he thought I had influence with Hilary Sloane. But all this, as you say, is assumption."

"Yes—but it's assumption, old lad, that fits a very complicated set of facts. I don't pretend that I could go straightaway and prove it. If it's right, however, we'll be able to bring it home all right. Eston has associates in a game of this kind and that will be the weak spot in his armor. I never did believe that there was anything in the proverb in there being honor among thieves. If crooks could trust one another the world would be hopelessly at their mercy and Scotland Yard worse than useless."

Silverdale flung the butt of his cigarette through the window and rolled a new one. The situation revealed was, as Garfield said, a working hypothesis and might very well shatter to pieces when brought face to face with practical facts. Still it gave a reason, a motive for many happenings which had hitherto seemed purposeless. There was only one point on which Garfield had not touched. If Eston thought Hilary was Saxon's wife—or rather widow—there was one obvious way certain to occur to him by which he could make sure of Saxon's fortune. It might be part of his plan to marry her—or attempt to marry her. Jimmie thought it highly unlikely that she would ever agree, whatever pressure was brought to bear upon her. That pressure could be brought to bear, there was no doubt. He set his shoulders squarely and his lips pressed to a thin, straight line as he contemplated the possibilities of the methods that a man such as Eston might Dring to bear on a girl like Hilary.

"What do you think?" asked Garfield.

"I think," said Jimmie decisively, "that the sooner we lay hands on Hilary, the better it will be for all of us. I hate to think of what may be happening to her at this very moment. We've got to find her—quick."

"I am rather inclined to agree with you," observed Garfield.

XIII

A PUNT shot out from the dappled shadow of willows fringing the backwater and slid slowly by a solitary flower-covered house-boat. It was a house-boat such as may be seen on almost any reach of the Thames in summer, with its upper deck fringed with geraniums and calceolarias, its windows daintily curtained and a flanneled figure lounging in a deck chair. It lay hidden from the main stream, yet not so far away but that it was easily accessible.

The man in the deck chair dropped his book and yawned. As he stretched himself, however, a close observer might have seen that he never took his eyes from the punt until it disappeared round the bend. A few seconds later, a double-oared rowing skiff appeared from the opposite direction and moored inconspicuously some two hundred yards from the house-boat; so inconspicuously that it would scarce be noticed from the latter craft through the green promontory behind which it sheltered, unless one were looking for it. The man on the house-boat frowned.

"They're at work," he muttered. "I was a blamed fool to give the show away, as I did. We've been under observation for the last three hours. Well, we'll see."

He rose languidly and entered the little saloon in which two girls were seated. Hilary was reading and Nora was bending over a watercolor sketch. Both looked up as he entered.

"Well, ladies," he observed, "you will be sorry to learn that your stay in this idyllic spot is drawing to a close. As a humble old friend of mine used to remark: 'The 'ounds is out.'"

A light of apprehension leapt into Nora's green eyes.

"The police—" she began.

He nodded. "Our worthy friends from Scotland Yard reinforced, no doubt, by the alert mind of our young friend Silverdale are on to us. They have got us picketed and are playing a waiting game just now. I fancy they are not quite sure enough to pounce. If you go outside, Miss Dring, and look carefully to the right, you will see a boat near the bank with two men in it."

Nora rose with a swish of skirts and passed out, a charming figure in white, to view the watchers in their seclusion. Eston turned with a smile to Hilary. "This rather forces my hand, Miss Sloane. It will be awkward if they should take it into their heads to try to effect an arrest."

Hilary placed one hand at the back of her neck and looked up at him. She was all in white—a picture of summer. A hint of amusement flickered round her lips. "Yes," she answered placidly. "I suppose it would be awkward—for you. I don't see why you should drag me into your sudden upheaval of conscience."

"My dear young lady," he said suavely. "You know as well as I do that if I stood aside and let matters take their course, you would be in peril of a very alarming experience. Do you realize that you are suspected of the murder of Sir Harold Saxon? Do you understand?"

The girl smiled, a half-mocking, cynical smile. "I understand—that," she said. "There are lots of things I don't understand. Why, for instance, you should take such a very great interest in a comparative stranger—so great an interest that you abduct me and make me a prisoner on this boat. I know that you employ men to watch me night and day. Is this just pure altruism on your part to help a suspected murderess to escape, or what? It has been a little episode and I've enough of the in me to have enjoyed it in a sense, but I'm a little tired of it now. Really, I'm not afraid of the police—are you?"

There was challenge in her gray eyes—a contemptuous challenge which somehow worried him.

Threats, tears, entreaties—he would have known how to meet them, but this cool, nonchalant attitude was calculated to disconcert even so adroit a man as Eston.

"You're a cool hand," he said admiringly. "Jove, what a pair we should make—you and I together, Hilary. We'd have the world at our feet."

"You flatter me," she said scornfully.

"I mean it," he declared earnestly. "Hilary, you're in a tight corner. There is not a soul on earth that you can rely on to get you out except myself. I know that you have probably got some lingering sentiment in your mind for that newspaper fellow—for Jimmie Silverdale. Put him out of your mind. He doesn't amount to anything and he's hand in glove with Scotland Yard. Don't," his voice sunk to an impressive whisper, "don't under-estimate what you're up against if you don't stand in with me. At the best it's a shameful notoriety—every catch-penny rag in the country yelping at you as the woman suspected of murdering Saxon; at the worst an ignominious death. Marry me, Hilary, and play the game with me—the big, bold game that we'll pull off together. It's your only chance, girl!"

Whether he was acting or not, he seemed terribly in earnest. He seized her hand, and at the physical contact she sprang to her feet, wrenching herself free. Her eyes were blazing but she held herself well under command. She realized that it would be a fatal error in tactics to lose her temper.

"You will keep your hands off me," she ordered sharply.

"Forgive me," he muttered silkily. "I am not responsible for myself when I am in your presence, Hilary. You madden me—I want you—"

"That will do," she broke in. "I don't know which I dislike most—your love-making or your veiled threats. I'm not a child, Mr. Eston. In future, you will keep your hands from me. I'm in your power for the moment but a time will come—" She broke off and trilled with a merry burst of laughter. "Oh, I 'm talking like the heroine in a melodrama. Yet I don't see why not. This is all sheer melodrama and you make an admirable villain. If you'd only tell me what it is all about—but leave out my Christian name, please. I have a prejudice in favor of that being used only by friends of my own sex."

He took a glance through the muslin curtains across the cool sheen of the river and made up his mind to play his hand for all it was worth. "You said just now that you were not afraid of the police. Do you mean that?"

"Mean it? Of course I mean it. Why shouldn't I?"

"You accuse me of keeping you a prisoner," he went on quietly. "You say I've abducted you and am holding you against your will. Very welL The police are there,"—he pointed across the river—"close at hand, well within earshot. You have only to raise your voice and you will bring them here."

It was an audacious move, for Eston knew there was more than a chance she would take him at his word. She regarded him for a couple of seconds without replying. He had dared her and she was inclined to take him at his word. Yet though she would not have cared to admit it, the possibility of what might follow a cry daunted her.

"No," she said. "I will not."

His laugh rang through the little saloon—a laugh, as it seemed to her, half of mockery, half of relief. "No, of course you won't," he sneered. "Shall I tell you why you won't? You realize that what I have told you of its meaning is true."

She regarded him a little speculatively, her head poised sideways, her lips parted in a half smile. Something of this sort she had foreseen and she was well on her guard. For all the emotion she displayed they might have been engaged in some half-playful academic discussion. "My dear man," she countered and her voice was steady, "you are trying to frighten me with bogeys. I am not a child."

"No, you are not a child. I'll do you that credit—you

are certainly not a child. You are playing a deep game, my dear, for all your naive eyes and pink and white complexion. But you overlook one fact in this business—I hold the ace of trumps."

"Really?" she lifted her eyebrows in mock surprise.

"Yes, Miss Sloane, I hold you—ah," he hesitated a second as though to add emphasis to his next words. "I beg your pardon, perhaps I should not address you as Miss Sloane."

"If you must address me at all I see no reason why you shouldn't. To be frank, you rather bore me; I'd rather you were dangerous than a bore." She swung a white shoe idly to and fro. "Your ace of trumps will fail you, you know."

"I think not," he declared. "If you will continue to push your head in the sand I must disillusion you as to what I know—and what the police probably know. I apologized for calling you Miss Sloane just now. Should I have said Lady Saxon?"

Hilary Sloane's foot came abruptly to the floor. Astonishment, bewilderment was in her face. "Lady Saxon," she repeated.

His lean fingers were drumming steadily on the tablecloth, while he studied her face searchingly. "Why not? "he asked calmly. "Legally and technically I think you are entitled to the name. I must congratulate you on your attitude at this moment. You are a picture of innocent astonishment. Did anyone ever tell you that you have all the qualities of a consummate actress? If I were not sure—if I did not have definite proof—you would almost shake my faith in myself."

She laughed. "So I'm Lady Saxon, am I! This is your ace of trumps. I suppose this explains your vivid and paternal interest in me? I am sorry I called you a bore. Your qualities of imagination are sometimes entertaining. Please continue."

"I will," he said grimly. "You married Harold Saxon when he was a nonentity. For some reason you lived apart when he came to this country to build up a fortune as well as a title. You will probably be interested to a large extent in the fortune he acquired. Let me be blunt. Whether you live to enjoy it or not depends upon me, upon my silence and upon my aid."

"I see." She was still smiling. "I am Lady Saxon, I am a murderess. I am likely to inherit a huge fortune. That's what it all comes to, doesn't it?"

"Put it that way, if you like."

She glanced at him from the corner of her eyes. "Do you know what an accessory after the fact is, Mr. Eston?" He scowled at her. Without waiting for a reply, she went on. "It is very noble of you to risk penal servitude in your endeavor to shield me—a widow with a past, a murderess!"

"Let's have done with this nonsense," he said peremptorily.

"It's not nonsense, I'm just analyzing the position. You want to marry me. Surely I am entitled to consider things? It would be an injustice to saddle so chivalrous a man as yourself with a sordid, wretched woman such as I. Don't you agree with me? And yet I see no way for you to acquire the money without me. It's a problem, isn't it?"

Eston studied her doubtfully. His cleverness, all of the many years' experience of human nature which he had gained failed him in his attempt to diagnose what was at the back of the girl's mind. She had him guessing—and he was a man who hated to be in doubt.

"Does that mean that you climb down?—that you are agreeing to marry me after all?"

She swept him a low curtsy. "It means," she said, "that, much though I appreciate your generous offer, I must decline with thanks."

He turned abruptly on his heel and swung round again as he reached the doorway, with an expression not pleasant to see.

"I'll have you on your knees yet, whining for me to lift a finger. We'll see who's top dog—and don't you forget it!

Meanwhile, you had better get ready to leave this place in half an hour."

Her features puckered in a grimace that was lost on Eston as he closed the door.

"Top dog," she murmured. "Yes, we'll see who does come out top dog. If I can keep my temper and my wits, I think I know who it will be."

XIV

VANITY was not one of Eston's faults. He was too big
a crook to let wounded feelings affect his judgment as a
general rule. Yet he was hurt. His confidence in himself,
that natural equanimity and confidence that comes to
every citizen of the world—had been shaken. He prided
himself on his judgment of men and women, but Hilary
Sloane had him guessing. He was very much more
puzzled, perhaps, than he would have cared to admit.

He had her in a cleft stick—he could break her as he
could a twig—but her attitude suggested either that she
did not realize, or that she did not care. It was impossible
to believe that she did not realize. She was too clever a
girl for that. He had left her no loophole for
misunderstanding. Either she was staking everything
upon a colossal bluff, or she was acting upon some
knowledge that had not reached him.

Eston never played a small game, save on those
exceptional cases, when it was a question oi bread and
butter—as a great actor or artist may at times descend to
pot-boilers. It was a big stake here. He had planned his
effects broadly. None knew better than he that some
small trivial detail might wreck his whole scheme, and it
was only force of circumstances that had made him bring
off his coup before he was entirely ready. The more he
cogitated, the keener grew his conviction, that he did not
hold the entire threads. If Silverdale had been
reasonable, if he had been able to pick up anything when
he had encountered Garfield and the journalist! He
clenched his fists and swore softly to himself.

Now things were getting red-hot. He had made a point
of seeing the morning's papers, and was quick to realize
what he was up against. The whole world was looking for

Hilary Sloane —a fact of which she was at the moment ignorant but which, sooner or later, she would know. Moreover, the house-boat was no longer a secure hiding-place. At any moment—he glanced over his shoulder towards the white-flanneled men in the skiff—the police might pounce. If he only knew what they knew, how much they knew—his features contorted in a spasm of irritation—he would know whether to put up a fight or a bluff.

The world seldom appreciates the qualities that make a great criminal. He has often to conduct a fight against overwhelming odds. The strength and weakness of his position is the fact that he must conduct his operations in secret. He dare not let his identity or his real purpose be known. He is blindfolded against antagonists using every resource of science and organization—a very Ishmael of civilization. He stakes his knowledge of human nature against a solid system and when he wins out, he has earned any satisfaction he gets.

By nature and by inclination, Eston was a fighter. He fought, as the Germans fought, for an end, and regardless of means. He wanted money; he wanted power; he wanted ease and security. The simplest, most direct way had seemed to him to be to steal. The chief difference between him and a casual burglar or pickpocket was one of method. Brains tell in crime, as in other branches of professional livelihood, and to brains Eston had wedded a long and varied experience. Audacity—audacity—always audacity. The old French saying had won him through tight places again and again. Others may have suffered, but always Eston went free.

He paced the deck once or twice, turning matters over in his mind, when he became aware that Nora Dring had disappeared. He searched the bank with his eyes up and down the fringe oi shrubs and trees that ran for fifty yards each side of the house-boat.

"Miss Dring—Nora!"

There was no answer. He muttered a curse beneath

his breath. Women were the very devil and all. If a girl had wanted to vanish, she could not have chosen a more inopportune time.

He strode across the plank connecting the boat with the bank and, alert and wary, moved through the shrubs to where, a few hundred yards away, a five-barred gate gave access to a quiet lane. There was no sign of Nora Dring, but a man was seated on the gate, as it seemed idly contemplating nature, and smoking a particularly vile brier pipe. A pair of shrewd brown eyes rested for a moment on Eston. It was an entirely natural spot for a tired wayfarer to rest, yet Eston knew that this man, who, in his ill-fitting flannels and boater, might have been a shop assistant spending a quiet half-holiday, was not there by accident, any more than the men in the rowing skiff, who commanded the river approach to his retreat, were solely bent on pleasure. He admired efficacy, whether it told against him or not, and he knew now that every line of the retreat was watched. He wondered whether the man on the gate was alone; he knew that on this kind of thing detectives usually hunted in pairs. If, however, as seemed likely, Nora Dring had passed that way, it was highly probable that the other police officer was keeping an unobtrusive eye on her.

He nodded amiably.

"Do you chance to have seen a young lady come this way? She left me a little while back, and I've missed her."

The other removed his pipe from his mouth.

"I've seen no one," he declared. "I've only been here this last minute or two. Probably she went out before then."

"Thanks. It's likely," agreed Eston, accepting what he knew to be a lie.

Leaning against the gate, with folded arms, he eyed the road up and down, and again lifted his voice in a shout. If Nora Dring was within earshot, which was doubtful, she made no response. Eston stretched his arms.

"No luck! I wonder where she's got to?"

"Don't know, I'm sure," said the other, staring straight in front of him with absorption. Eston was not easily put off. If Nora was out of earshot, it was likely that any shadower would be also.

"Beautiful day, isn't it?" said he, making the opening gambit of a man willing for desultory conversation.

"Grand," admitted the other shortly.

"I fancy we may get a thunder-storm before long. This is much too good to last."

Eston's right hand was fumbling in the pocket of his jacket.

"Yes, that's so."

The watcher did not seem much in the mood for conversation. He shifted his legs to a more comfortable grip of the gate, and puffed away serenely, the while his gaze wandered far away over Eston's head. He was more absorbed than ever in the view.

"Boating?" asked Eston.

"Not exactly. Just down for an hour or two."

"Well, it's a beautiful part of the river. If you see a young lady, you might tell her that I've been looking for her. My name's Eston."

He turned, as if to go, but he was watching very closely. The man on the gate seemed quite uninterested. If he recognized the name, he showed no sign. He nodded, and puffed a cloud of smoke.

"Right-oh! I'll tell her."

Eston had taken one pace back towards the house-boat when he wheeled swiftly. There was a sheen of blue as he lifted his hand. The man. on the gate found himself looking down the blue barrel of an automatic pistol. He pulled his pipe from his mouth, and remained a picture of amazement.

"What the dev—!"

"Cut that!" ordered Eston sharply. "I'm in a hurry! Get down from that gate! Hear me? Get down!"

"If it's money you want," protested the other man,

"I've only got a matter of ten shillings—"

Eston's left hand gripped him by the arm, while the muzzle of his pistol was stealing within a couple of inches of his face. The man clambered down hastily, dropping his pipe as he did so.

"Don't argue," insisted Eston. "I'm a desperate man, and you'll be wise to do exactly as you're told. I'm ready to take a chance. Now, march straight in front of you, and don't look back or make a sound. Get me?"

"I get you. I'd like my pipe, if you don't mind. It's a good pipe, and I'd hate to lose it."

He stooped, fingers outstretched towards the brier, and suddenly, sprawling at full length, grasped Eston's legs. Had Eston not been on the alert, it is possible the ruse might have succeeded. His fingers closed on the trigger, but in that fraction of a second sanity returned to him. The sound of a shot would be too risky, for investigation by those other watchers on the river would be near and prompt. He reversed the weapon as he dodged, and the butt fell heavily on the prostrate man's head. He gave a soft, sobbing sigh, and lay limp.

"The darned fool!" grunted Eston, and wiped the weapon carefully with a handful of grass. Then he lifted the unconscious man and bore him to a heavy clump of gorse, where he deposited his burden. Then deftly and swiftly he made a search of the other's pockets. It revealed little that he did not know—a watch, a little money, a few private letters, a police diary and notebook, and a warrant-card, such as is carried by all men of the Criminal Investigation Department.

"I thought so," commented Eston grimly, and transferred the letters to his own pockets. One never knows when such things may be useful. Besides, it was quite possible that the diary—that little book which every detective is expected to keep posted, so that he may account for his time and expenses to his superiors—might contain a hint of things Eston wished to know. He did not, however, attach tremendous expectations to this. It was improbable that any of Garfield's subordinates would know the grand strategy of the case. They would be used only for minor tactics.

Eston stripped the braces, and took a handkerchief from the senseless man, and with these and his own handkerchief contrived to tie and gag his victim roughly but effectively. Then, dusting himself with care he climbed the gate, and strolled down the road. He had proceeded, perhaps, a quarter of a mile when he met Nora Dring, hatless and cool.

"I have been looking for you," he said tartly. "Where have you been?"

She thrust a hand through his arm, and they began to walk back.

"I wanted to see Velvet," she said. "I gathered that, in the circumstances, you are not going to stay here too long. I thought it advisable to take time by the forelock. The car will be ready in ten minutes."

"Good girl!" he said approvingly. "I think it is time we made a move."

"There's another thing," she went on quietly. "We're watched from this side. I'm being shadowed at this moment. There was another man on the gate. You must have noticed him."

"Yes, I noticed him. You can strike him out of the account for a little while. I'm more concerned about a gentleman who's following you."

"He's about a hundred yards behind us at the moment," she went on. "Velvet is bringing on the car, and Jim is following our follower. "

He lit a cigarette and shadowed his face.

"I've told Hilary to be ready to leave the boat," he said. "I'll get you to go back and hurry her up. I don't think somehow that our friends in the skiff intend any action at the moment, unless their hand is forced. You bring her back here, and Jim and I will deal with this other gentleman from Scotland Yard."

A bend in the road shielded them for a moment from a

view of their shadower. Eston paused by a big oak so that
its trunk concealed him from anyone advancing towards
them. The girl went on.

It was a different type of man to that he had already
dealt with who presently came into Eston's line of vision.
A massive giant of a man, rugged of face and frame, a
dirty cap on a thick, uncombed head of hair, unshaven,
and with a brilliant blue muffler knotted round his
throat.

Eston moved from his concealment.

The big individual slouched on, apparently unheeding,
until a detaining hand touched him on the shoulder.

"You have been annoying a lady friend of mine," said
Eston, a note of sternness in his voice. "What do you
mean by it?"

"Lemme alone, guv'nor," said the man. "I ain't
interfered with no lidy friend of yours. What d'yer take
me for?"

Eston saw a figure round a bend towards them—the
man Nora Dring had referred to as Jim. Away in the
distance came the faint hoot of a motor-car.

"I take you for a condemned fool," he said. "That's
enough of it—understand! This is where you get off, my
friend, if you don't want to fall into the hands of the
police. You don't come any further down this road. Clear
out!"

The detective hesitated. Eston was treating him as
any man might treat a tramp, and that was what the
detective supposed that he was believed to be. It was his
duty to keep observation, as the official phrase goes, on
Eston and his party. He had followed Nora Dring because
she came to the house-boat. She was obviously on her way
back to her comrade, and he would be certain to pick her
up. It was his plain duty to drop her and keep an eye on
Eston himself.

"You've got the wrong end of the stick, guv'nor," he
protested. "Still, it's all one to me. I'll turn round the
other way if you want me to."

"I'll walk with you a bit of the way," said Eston, and pushed his hand through the other's arm. Jim was close upon them now—a wiry, bronzed young man, with America as the country of his origin shrieking all over him, from his round hat, his loose, long-skirted coat, and his wide, creased trousers and his small boots with the toes curving inward. Jim was a "strong arm"—an ally useful on occasions like this. He was walking swiftly, and he caught Eston's almost imperceptible nod as they neared each other.

The attack was so swift and so sudden that the detective probably never realized exactly how it happened. Eston had disentangled his arm, and with a tigerish movement sprang on him from behind with a throttle-hold that choked back the first alarmed cry. His arm was round the other's mouth and nose, his knee in his back, and Jim had his hands in the detective's hair, pulling him forward.

The struggle was sharp but short. It was a matter of seconds before the man was as helpless as a baby, face downwards in the dust. From somewhere in an inside pocket Jim produced a short, yielding length of material about an inch in diameter and eighteen inches long. A sandbag is a deadly weapon in experienced hands. Eston drew back, and his companion administered what seemed to be the slightest tap on the back of the neck.

The struggles of the detective ceased, and Eston rose.

"Not overdone it, have you?" he asked, more in a tone of casual curiosity than of one doubtful whether he has or has not assisted at murder.

"I should smile," said Jim, scornful at the aspersion on his dexterity, running his ringers over the sandbag and stowing it away in his pocket. "The guy won't know what's given him a headache in a couple of hours' time."

XV

ESTON 's reasons for assuming that there would be
no immediate move on the part of the police were sound
as far as they went. He had reasoned that they would be
content to watch for the time being since they had not
paused when they came within view of their quarry.
There was only one flaw in his reasoning. That was
Detective-Sergeant Wade. Wade had all that day been
acting as Garfield's deputy during the latter's absence,
and had obeyed instructions by having an eye kept on
Eston until Garfield should decide to take active steps.
Wade was enjoying the relief from routine duty in town,
and since he saw a way to combine business with
pleasure, he was one of the white-flanneled figures in the
skiff that had aroused attention from the house-boat.

Now Wade had a high appreciation of Eston's
capacity—in ingenuity of resource he knew himself far
outmatched, but he had a bull-dog tenacity that served
him very often nearly as well as delicate finesse. He was
not an easy man to throw off once he had got his teeth
fixed. So it was that he did not altogether rely on the men
who were watching the landward side of Eston's retreat.

Through a pair of powerful binoculars he had watched
Nora Dring leave the house-boat. He became somewhat
uneasy when he saw Eston follow her some time later.
When he saw Nora return, and in a little leave with
Hilary, carrying a small hand bag, he deemed that things
might be happening of which it would be well he should
know. Of course there were a couple of good men the
other side—but—well, it was always as well to be sure!

Nora, over her shoulder, caught a glimpse of the skiff
pulling across the stream, and smothered an exclamation.

"They've seen us, Hilary! They're coming across! We must hurry—oh, hurry!" she exclaimed.

They broke into a run, and as they did so Wade's suspicions were fanned to a flame. He and his companion pulled savagely, but Wade's skill was not equal to his energy, and he caught a crab in midstream and only the sheerest luck prevented him taking an involuntary ducking.

"It's a get-away!" he snapped. "By the great blue snake, the guv'nor will be hopping mad if we lose 'em!"

But the girls were well beyond the gate before the two detectives landed, and no amount of sprinting would have served to overtake them in any reasonable distance. Nevertheless, Wade and his companion made the effort. They were in time to see a powerful motor-car pick up the two and disappear in a cloud of dust. If Wade had been less stirred, he would have recognized the futility of men on foot chasing a fast car. Yet he held doggedly on, hoping, perhaps, for some remote chance. The car was long out of sight when they reached the main road into which the by-lane led. Wade collapsed, panting, to the side of a ditch.

"A clean get-away!" he gasped. "And me thinking we 'd got 'em corked up nice and tight. Not even got the number of their car—though that would be a fat lot of use. I expect it's faked!"

His companion was gazing up the dusty, white strip of road towards Twyford.

"They're coming back!" he announced.

"No such luck," groaned Wade, but stirred himself so far as to rise and watch the cloud of dust that was rapidly approaching them. It resolved itself into a big four-seater, and drew to a standstill as it neared them.

"Here's luck," said Wade. "It's the guv'nor."

Jimmie Silverdale was at the wheel, and seated by his side, cool and imperturbable, a flower in his buttonhole, was Garfield. He nodded to his "aide."

"Got 'em bottled up safe still, eh?"

Wade groaned.

"Did you pass a big car going hell for leather a few minutes ago!"

Both Silverdale and Garfield jumped to the situation in a flash. As simultaneous ejaculations burst from them, Wade wagged his head in assent.

"That's them! They 've slipped us!"

"Have they?" said Garfield resolutely. "We'll see! Jump in, Wade!"

Jimmie was already backing the big car round. Wade turned to his companion on their fruitless run.

"Slip back to see what has become of our other two men. I'll get along with Mr. Garfield. Right you are, sir! Go ahead!"

Garfield left Jimmie to himself and took his seat in the tonneau with Wade.

"I'd blame some men for a business like this," he said, "but I know you've done everything that could be done. Tell me about it. Let her out, Jimmie, we've got to overtake them!"

"If we'd only thought," answered Jimmie. "We had 'em practically in our hands."

"No good crying over spilt milk," said the inspector. "We couldn't hold up every car we met on the off chance that Eston was in it. He'd, have a lively time! We've got a sporting chance of catching them. They wouldn't expect us to be off the mark so soon. Now, then, Wade!"

Jirnme pulled at the lever, and the great car slid smoothly forward, gaining momentum with every inch. For once all such things as speed limits were forgotten. All that mattered was overtaking the fugitives—if, indeed such a thing was possible.

‘   ›   ‘   ›

‘

Given a good car not too distinctive in appearance, with a start that enables it to get well out of sight on a network of roads, and the odds are against any successful pursuit, even in an equally good car. In something less than half an hour the futility of the chase became apparent. Since this is a plain story, an apology is due to the reader for the failure of Garfield and Silverdale to follow up a trail that would have been inevitable—to the reader of detective novels. They might, for instance, have followed the distinctive imprint of Eston's tires on the road— if there had been any distinctive imprint, which there was not. Their inquiries, necessarily vague, met with still vaguer replies. At every crossroads they lost time, and there was no certainty, after all their trouble, that they were not moving in an opposite direction to that taken bv Eston and his companions.

Silverdale pulled the car up, and looked over his shoulder at the detective.

"It's no go!" he proclaimed ruefully. "We're up against it!"

Garfield got out of the body of the car, and resumed his seat by Silverdale.

"If we had happened to recognize them as we passed," he said. "however, it's the luck of the game. We'll get back to Twyford, Jimmie."

They reached the spot where they had picked up Wade in less than an hour from the time they had left it and made their way through the lane leading to the house-boat. Among the detectives now concentrated on that flower bedecked craft were two bruised and disconcerted men who were looking forward none too eagerly to their interview with the chief inspector.

He listened quietly while they told their stories in the blunt, matter-of-fact way that police officers affect in their relations with their superiors.

"The plain fact is," he commented, "that Eston was too clever for both of you. He played you for a couple of nickers."

Garfield took off his coat and got to business. It needed no practiced eye to see that the departure of the fugitives had been taken without pre-arrangement.

Presently the inspector's eye lit on a white square on a small table. He picked it up.

"Hallo, Jimmie!" he said. "This looks as if it belonged to you!"

He handed over a small envelope. Jimmie turned it over in his hand. It was addressed:

J. Silverdale, Esq.
Very private. By Courtesy of the Police."

"Becoming a convenient postman for a change," said Garfield. "I'll hazard a bet that it's from your little lady friend, Miss Hilary Sloane!"

Silverdale tore it open.

"You're right, it's from Hilary."

XVI

DURING the temporary absence of Nora Dring and Eston from the house-boat, Hilary had used her opportunities. She knew that once they had accomplished their flight, it would only be a matter of time before the police would be at their river hiding-place. And something brought it home to her that with the police would come Jimmie Silverdale. She could have given few logical reasons for this assumption. She just knew, instinctively. She had penned her message in wild feverish haste, always on the alert for the return of either of her companions and she had concluded hurriedly.

Jimmie Silverdale seated himself on a small table, his legs swinging, and began to read. Garfield jerked his head peremptorily and the other detectives moved silently out of the tiny saloon, leaving the inspector and the journalist alone.

"What does she say?" asked Garfield. "That won't be exactly a confidential love letter, if I'm any judge."

A slight tinge of red crept into the other's sallow cheek. He shook his head laughingly. "No," he agreed. "You shall read it in a moment." He resumed his perusal of the letter.

"My dear Jimmie," Hilary had begun. Then apparently, on second thought, she had crossed out the Jimmie and substituted "Mr. Silverdale." Jimmie noticed and smiled thoughtfully.

"What can you think of me?" she went on. "If these last two or three days have been a waking nightmare to me, I have only myself to blame, but you, to whom I owe so much, may also have suffered through my lack of trust in you, or perhaps through too much trust in someone else. They have gone to arrange for us again to take flight, and I may have to cut this letter short at any instant. Jimmie, the time has come when I must trust you fully and frankly. You are the only person on whom I can rely to cut the dreadful tangle by which I am surrounded.

"I know how black circumstances must seem to you of all people, but I swear to the powers above that I have had no willing complicity in the terrible crime with which I seem to be associated. Sir Harold Saxon was a name to me— a name only—until the moment when you, of all People! told me that he had been murdered and that I was a suspect in the eyes of the police. From that stunning second, I have been haunted by an intolerable dilemma—for I had pledged my word. Now I consider myself released.

"When I asked you to spirit Nora and myself secretly from town, I was doing so at her request. She had come to the studio after a night's absence distraught beyond measure and begged me to help her. "We had been friends for many years and as I thought had no secrets from each other. Now she was faced with some awful calamity of which she would give me no hint beyond the fact that the police would probably be seeking her. She clung to me like a frightened child, weeping and beseeching that I would not leave her. What could I do? We had been friends—with a friendship even exceeding that of sisters—for years. So I promised and sent for you. The secret was not my own. I could tell you nothing.

"It was next morning when you called for us that I realized part of the possible truth, but even then I could not credit that she, any more than myself, could be a possible murderess. I had to play the game by her, Jimmie. Even when I saw that you misunderstood, I had to play the game.

"There are many things dark to me in this story, sequences that perhaps you may be able to fill, gaps that you may bridge with your fuller knowledge and opportunities for inquiry. You said that Sir Harold Saxon had a photograph of mine. How that came to be I cannot tell. I never set eyes on the man alive in my life.

"My acquaintance with Eston dates back scarcely a fortnight. I met him first with Nora at a small art exhibition, and she introduced as a very old friend of hers. We dined together all three of us that night, and once afterwards at Nora's request, I joined them at a small restaurant. I remember being left alone with Eston for a little and that he went over to speak to a man. I now know the man to be a hanger-on of his — a man who is assisting him in whatever scheme he has on at present and who is called Velvet Fred.

"There was not the slightest reason for me to be suspicious of Eston, yet it is clear enough now that we were and are pawns in some very deep and wide game that he is playing — a game which with your help I shall ultimately fathom.

"It was after you had seen us off from Paddington that I began to realize what a great change the last few days had brought over Nora. After what you had said, I had to regard her with fresh eyes, for all the damning facts which to an outsider told against me were tenfold deadly against her. Yet somehow, Jimmie, I revolted against regarding her as — that! She cross-examined me about you on the way down and I am afraid we had some unpleasantness.

"But it was not until we reached Twyford that I began to realize that other people — particularly Eston — were concerned. There Eston intercepted us, and there she threw off the mask. To all intents and purposes, I was given to understand that I was their prisoner—that any attempt at defiance would be met by the story that I was a lunatic.

"I had enough confidence in myself to face a public scene if necessary—but a public scene there would have meant the probable revelation of my identity and you had said enough to let me know that I stood in peril of arrest by the police should they once know where to find me. I was a coward. I could not face that sordid and unnecessary publicity. So I accepted things as they were, but I managed to get a wire sent off to you.

"It was to this boat that I was brought. There was no physical constraint upon me, though through the silky, oily manner of Eston, I could read his full intention not to hesitate if need be. In some way I was essential to a great conspiracy which was on foot. At that time I had not the remotest idea what it might mean. If Nora and Eston were concerned with the murder of Sir Harold Saxon, why did they trouble themselves about me? I thought then that they might believe I should be a witness against them—but even so, why should they handicap themselves? Three people are easier to trace than two.

"Nora has to this moment made no explanation; indeed her manner has been, if not coldly brutal, at least repellent. She has given me to understand that I must obey orders, if necessary. Eston is suave and, I fear, dangerous. Behind, all this business, there is some mystery, some motive that I cannot penetrate. I feel baffled, like one groping vainly in the dark.

"Less than an hour ago, he paid me the compliment of offering me marriage. I am afraid I did one indiscreet thing with such a man—I laughed at him. He pointed out that the police were, even then, within eyeshot of us and that they believed me to be guilty of a terrible crime. Now Eston is a shrewd man and I am not conceited enough to believe that he is taking the risks he must be taking for the sake of my beautiful eyes! There is a nigger in the wood-pile somewhere, and through Eston's hurt vanity, when I mocked him, I caught a glimpse —the merest glimpse.

"This man may, or may not, believe that I am a guilty woman. He certainly believes that I have been closely associated with the late Saxon—that I am in fact his widow. It all sounds wildly fantastic and incredible, doesn't it, Jimmie? It would be funny, if it were not so tragic! So this abduction—if it is an abduction—has been arranged for the sake of marrying me off to a man who wishes to lay his fingers on a colossal fortune left by Sir Harold Saxon. The scheme has more intricate complications, perhaps, than the bald statement can suggest and I am not quite clear how far Nora is involved, except that she is acting as a sort of female jailer upon me.

"I am ashamed to confess that Eston makes an astute guess at my feelings and my fears for, during this afternoon's scene, he challenged me to raise my voice and call the police who were watching. I wanted to, and yet somehow I dare not. I am just a little coward. If I am to be talked about as I realize I must be in the end, I want to clear myself of the faintest taint of suspicion. By remaining for the moment with Nora and Eston, I may be enabled to reach the heart of the mystery.

"I hear Nora returning. I must stop. Love

—H."

Jimmie turned the four pages of closely written letter paper over and over and stared blankly at Garfield. The chief inspector held out a hand impatiently and took the missive. Silverdale rolled himself a cigarette and striking a match on the sole of his boot, smoked in silence while Garfield with wrinkled brows digested Hilary's message.

"Well?" he asked at last.

"Pity she hadn't time to be more detailed," observed the detective. "She's a clever young lady and Eston apparently has found her a bigger handful than he anticipated. She has put her finger on the heart of the mystery."

Silverdale elevated expressive eyebrows. "A conspiracy to grab all the money Saxon made?"

"Not the slightest doubt of it. Eston obviously believes that she is Lady Harold Saxon, which is one of the points at which his cleverness is going to lead him into trouble.

Equally certain is the fact that he feels confident—or probably knows for certain—that Miss Sloane had nothing to do with the murder."

The journalist surveyed his companion with a slightly puzzled air. "I don't quite get that," he said. "If Eston, as is the most likely hypothesis, either killed Saxon himself or knows who did, of course he realizes that Hilary is innocent. But there is nothing in her letter to suggest that."

Garfield wore a slightly superior smile. He loved a little mystification. "Did it escape you, Jimmie, that Miss Sloane tells how he offered to marry her?"

"From all I know of Eston he wouldn't worry much whether his wife had a little thing like murder on her conscience."

"No? I am surprised at your ignorance of law, Jimmie. The moral side might not weigh with Eston at all, but other things would. A murderer cannot benefit from the death of his victim. If Hilary Sloane really had killed Harold Saxon, even if she were his wife, she could not legally obtain a penny of his estate. She would be barred from any benefit. Now, Eston wants to marry her because it will give him a finger in the loot. Therefore he is confident she has a claim."

"Thanks," said Jimmie dryly. "Meanwhile, perhaps you can make a guess at the lady who posed as Hilary Sloane when she married Saxon. It seems to me that the real Lady Saxon is a nigger in the wood-pile, as Hilary puts it."

"You don't want a microscope to see a barn door, Jimmie," observed Garfield with cryptic emphasis. "If dead certainties didn't so often turn out wrong, I'd make a little bet with you that I could give the lady's name. All that can be fixed up later. Meanwhile, I think we'll get back to town."

"Why?"

"Jimmie, neither your brain nor your observation is working at full pressure. You're too closely concerned with thinking of Hilary Sloane to do yourself full justice. See here?"

He placed a broad thumb-nail on the reverse of Hilary's envelope, where a tiny faintly penciled word could be seen.

"Miss Sloane got a hint of their destination at the last moment and passed it on for us," he went on.

The faintly penciled word was "London."

XVII

IF Eston had returned to London, there were ways and means of smoking him out. Part of the way back to town, Garfield occupied with pencil and paper. Long before they reached the western outskirts, he had drawn up instructions that on his arrival at Scotland Yard would be flashed over the private wires to every one of the two hundred police stations in the metropolis.

There are more than six hundred detectives in London, to say nothing of twenty thousand or more of the uniformed force. The instructions would automatically reach both, but it was on the Criminal Investigation Department that Garfield chiefly relied. Velvet Fred was, in the hackneyed phrase, well known to the police, and Jim, who had assisted in overpowering one of Garfield 's staff, was perhaps not less well known as "Knuckleduster" — a young international crook who had played a prominent part in several bank "hold-ups" in the United States, and was believed to be a leading spirit in several daring diamond robberies that had been effected in London.

Eston himself was only a name to most detectives; he was too clever to have ever become familiar to his natural enemies. Yet he had an awkward team to handle and if the police could only lay hands upon one of them, Garfield though no believer in third degree methods, yet had his own ways of persuasion.

Wade dropped off the car at Hammersmith. He was still in flannels and as there remained work for him to do that evening, he took the opportunity to change.

Later in the evening he turned up, a big-built, well-groomed man, in scrupulous evening dress over which he wore a light coat, in the West End. Half a dozen men west and east were on a similar quest to his—not excluding Garfield himself.

It is only on very exceptional occasions that detectives take a risk of facial disguise. The danger of using stage properties in public are too great. The real art of the detective is to camouflage himself so that he is not too obvious or obtrusive among his surroundings. Wade was going to rake the West End—there-fore he wore evening dress, but to anyone who knew him, he was just the same old Wade. If he had been going east, he would have had a dirty face, uncombed hair, untidy clothes and a muffler instead of a white collar.

Steadily, systematically, he worked his way through a series of saloon bars, restaurants, and night clubs. At most of them he was recognized; at very few did he refuse to take a drink with some friendly acquaintance or other. In some cases, indeed, he deliberately sought out men and invited them to drink with him. None refused, although in some cases, there was a shade of nervousness or constraint in their manner.

Wade drank much that night—chiefly ginger ale. For weeks afterwards the very thought of ginger ale sickened him. He had need of all his wits and he did not propose to drown them.

The men he selected to drink with were mainly associates, or possible intimates, of Velvet Fred or Knuckleduster. Wade had no airs. He might be a detective by profession, but this, he led those with whom he consorted to believe, was his night-off and he was just a good fellow among good fellows. Somehow, however, the conversation always swung round to either one or both of Eston's two assistants.

"Talking of that," Wade would observe genially, "I haven't heard of young Knuckleduster lately. How's he getting along? Well, here's how," and he would tilt his glass for another drink.

There is a hoary lie that there is honor among thieves. There is sometimes community of interest among thieves, but there is never honor. If there were, half the effectiveness of the detective forces of the world would be swept away. The backbone of all efficient detective work is the informant who sometimes volunteers information and is sometimes sought out as Wade was now seeking him. Seldom is there any reluctance to talk, save through fear of self-interest. Every man with whom Wade spoke that evening guessed that the detective's casual inquiry had something behind it, yet they were willing enough to talk so long as they themselves were not concerned.

Although the detective learned much of which, he made a mental note for future reference, he gained little to his immediate purpose for some hours. After a time, however, he strolled into a little public house in the network of streets between Oxford Street and Leicester Square and his eyes roved casually round the habitues.

A thin, weedy-looking youth caught that glance and immediately tried to melt among a group of people at one of the little tables. Wade smiled beneath his mustache and moved forward, looking anywhere but in the direction of the youth. The other sighed heavily with relief and tried to make an unobtrusive exit. He had about reached the door when Wade's hand fell on his shoulder and he started violently.

"Feeling pretty shy to-night, Jack. What are you trying to dodge me for?"

"Why, it's Mr. Wade!" Jack made an effort to conceal profound astonishment. "I wasn't trying to dodge you, sir. I was just going."

Wade tucked his arm through that of his victim and felt him shivering like a tracked rabbit. "So I see," he remarked pleasantly. "Well, there's no need to be in a hurry. Come and have one with me. Don't get wind up, my lad. I've got nothing against you just now."

"Sure, Mr. Wade," agreed Jack obsequiously, but disengaging his arm with a certain relief. "This is our man. What'll you 'ave?"

"Dry ginger, please," said Wade with inward nausea.

"I'm on the water wagon for a bit. Well, here's luck. How's things going with you?"

For a while conversation rambled round various points until at last Wade brought it to a definite question.

"Knuckleduster?" repeated Jack echoing the name. "Why, yes. He's about. I saw him tonight—not half an hour ago."

"Ah," Wade fingered his drink, outwardly with only perfunctory interest in the conversation, inwardly with tense watchfulness. "I was wondering what had happened to him. Where did you see him?"

"He was 'aving dinner with a baby doll up at Duller's in Piccadilly. We didn't speak. He seemed to be enjoying himself and I didn't want to interfere."

"That so? Glad he's managing to keep out of worse mischief," said Wade. "Well, I must be off, Jack. Early to bed and early to rise, you know—well, so long." He nodded and strolled out.

Duller's—which is not its real name—is a well-known restaurant, lavish of gilt and plate glass and beloved of suburban residents who "see life" in town once in a while. Wade kept his eyes open as he made his way thither, and delayed long enough to pick two plain-clothesmen off their patrols. He was not afraid to tackle Knuckleduster singlehanded, but he believed in taking precautions. If the crook caught sight of him too soon, he might make a bolt and it was as well to have the exits guarded.

Posting his men at the doors, he walked into the restaurant. The manager hastened forward to greet him. Wade was a well-known figure in places of this kind.

"Just lookin' for a friend of mine," said the detective. "It will be all right. You leave me alone."

It was on the basement floor that he at last found Knuckleduster. The young gentleman was seated at a table with the lady Wade's informant had described as a baby doll—a young lady with a very loud laugh, bright blue eyes and a somewhat transparent green frock. They had reached the liqueur stage and Knuckleduster was leaning across the table in an amorous attempt to make the lady take a sip from his creme-de-menthe when his jaw dropped and he stiffened in his chair.

"It's all right, Knuckleduster," said Wade, quietly dropping into a seat facing him. "I'm not a ghost."

There was a tinkle of glass as Knuckleduster's hand dropped heavily on the table. Yet he turned fierce fighting eyes on the detective. "I don't know you," he said defiantly. "Who in blazes are you, and what do you mean buttin' in onus like this?"

"Sock 'im in the jaw," advised his inamorata considerately.

"You've got a short memory, Knuckleduster," said Wade quietly. "My name's Wade. I'm a police officer. If the lady will be kind enough to leave us for a little while, I want to talk over some business with you. I've just come from Twyford," he added meaningly.

Knuckleduster's manner changed. "Oh, all right, Mr. Wade. Take no notice of Gwennie. She's liable to get excited. I'll just see her off the premises and then we'll have that talk."

"Sit right down," advised Wade quietly, but with a note of command in his voice. "Gwennie can find her own way out, I believe. You'll have to excuse us, my dear. This is all going to be very private."

"Right. Beat it, Gwen," ordered Knuckleduster, and settled himself defiantly in his chair.

The girl looked from one man to the other, and then, with a shrug of her shoulders and a shrill laugh, left them. Wade waited until she was out of earshot.

"I'm afraid I've got to take you in, Knuckleduster," he said.

"What for?" The other was brusque. "You ain't got nothing on me, an' you know it."

"I don't know what you call nothing," said Wade, "but if a little thing like beating up a police officer with a sandbag is nothing, you're on. I've got the goods on you, laddie, and it's no good putting up a squeal."

"You're a liar," said Knuckleduster bluntly. "I ain't been near Twyford to-day

and I can prove it."

"How did you know this assault took place at Twyford?" retorted Wade. "Don't be a condemned fool! Why, I can easily identify you—you and Eston and Velvet Fred. You're for it good and proper this time."

"I'll wait till you prove it," declared the other. He was the type of criminal that always believed the other man was bluffing until it came to a show-down.

"That may not be necessary," said Wade. "We've got it on you, and you were a sucker to come out to-night. If you're a sensible man, though, it won't need to go much farther. I'd hate to have to jug a man like you. Why can't we talk this over as between pals—you and I and the guv'nor?"

"Come across," said Knuckleduster suspiciously, "I don't take you."

Wade looked him squarely in the eyes. "Oh yes, you do," he answered firmly.

"You're asking me to squeal on Eston."

"I'm asking you to save your own skin. You're up against it, Knuckleduster, and you know it. Are you going with the rest of 'em or are you going to take a chance and give us a straight griffin?"

Knuckleduster's jaw set hard and he met Wade's eyes with a gaze as straight as his own. "Let's get this without any camouflage," he said. "If I cough up all I know, you'll let me make a clean get-away?"

Wade hesitated. It is a ticklish business getting a statement from a man implicated in a crime. The law is a jealous taskmaster.

"That all depends," he parried. "We might pass over this affair at Twyford if—if there's nothing else. The man isn't very seriously hurt."

"You gotta give me a clean sheet," persisted Knuckleduster.

"Not on your life," said Wade. "You can talk or you can

keep your trap shut, which you like. If you do the last, you'll take what's coming to you. What about it?"

"Nope!" declared Knuckleduster and shut his jaws tight.

"Well," said Wade smoothly, no trace of the chagrin he felt in his face, "I think we'd better be taking a walk along, Knuckleduster."

Arm in arm, like two intimate friends engaged in intimate conversation, the two men walked through the crowded dining-rooms and out of the restaurant.

XVIII

WHILE Knuckleduster cooled his heels in a cell at Grape Street police station Wade got busy on the telephone. His conversation with Garfield at Scotland Yard was short and correct. When he at last laid down the receiver he winked portentously at Rack, the divisional detective inspector who was standing at his elbow.

Rack scrutinized Wade's brick-red, immobile face steadily. "What's the game?" he demanded.

"Why"—Wade made a slight gesture in the open palms of his hands—"I take Knuckleduster up to the Yard myself. No other must. I don't take a cab or even handcuff him. Somewhere, somehow, while we are walking along together what happens—?"

"You take your eyes off him," broke in Rack smilingly.

"I've never lost a prisoner in my service," protested Wade solemnly, "but if he should chance to get away perhaps it wouldn't be a black mark against me. It might happen by luck that we'd have one or two people to follow him up. Knuckleduster will hot-foot it likely enough to wherever Eston's hang-out may be. It's all a chance but there are men keeping an eye on the little lady who brought him out to-night and we'll be able to pick him up again."

Knuckleduster Jim was surly when the deputation of two detectives accompanied by a jailer called on him in his cell. He felt that luck had played him a shabby trick. He was reclining in his shirt-sleeves on the thick board couch glumly-contemplating his stockinged feet when the door opened and shut again with a clang.

"Well, Jim," said Wade cheerfully. "Been thinking it over?"

Knuckleduster's gaze never shifted from his feet. He sat glum and silent.

"Come, my man," said Rack sharply. "Pull yourself together. We want to help you all we can."

.The prisoner gave a short, rasping laugh. "Say—I know all about that," he sneered.

Rack laid a gentle hand on his shoulder. "I hate to see a man go down because he's been played for a sucker by someone else. You've been let in for this. I guess that man you dropped across down at Twyford is pretty bad. Suppose you go down for attempted murder? Don't you hold out too much hopes on Eston, my lad. He may be in the pen himself to-morrow. Where will you be then? Better cough up and give us a hand."

Knuckleduster gave a contemptuous grunt. "Say your little piece," he sneered. "What am I?"

"Just a blame fool," retorted Rack. "You don't know who are your friends."

"Yes, I do." Jim's upper lip contorted so they could see his gums. "Your bluff don't go. Just you chew on that."

A quick glance passed between the two detectives. They realized that it was hopeless. Nothing they could do or say was likely to move the crook. His mind was plainly made up to defy them and when a criminal of Knuckleduster's caliber is obdurate coaxing and threats are equally futile.

"Get your boots and coat on," ordered Wade. "You're coming with me."

"Where to?" Jim swung himself up and languidly began to thrust one arm in the sleeve of his coat.

"Up to New Scotland Yard. Mr. Garfield wants to have a talk with you."

Slowly, rather as one voluntarily condescending to favor than as being forced to a course of action whether he willed or not, Knuckleduster assembled his attire. Rack pressed the bell that summoned the jailer and presently the judas hole that enabled one to see the interior of a cell from without, without opening the door, dropped back. At Rack's nod the jailer opened the door and they passed into the corridor, Wade's hand encircling the prisoner's wrist.

As they walked into the big bare charge-room Jim remembered something. "We coming back here?" he demanded.

"Sure thing," said Wade. "Why!"

"Only there's that stuff they took off me. I don't want to lose that."

The usual formality of search had been made when he had been brought to the charge-room, but Wade being in a hurry had not followed the usual custom of making an inventory. Nor had he confined himself to merely relieving the prisoner of knife, matches, and other articles with which he might do injury. He had simply cleared his pockets and left examination till later.

"You won't lose any of it that you are properly entitled to," said Wade. To the station sergeant in charge of the room he added, "You might send it along to the Yard if you don't mind—I'd like to look it over some time."

If Knuckleduster had suspected the elaborate arrangements that had been made in order that he might once again take the air of freedom, he might have been grateful. On the other hand, he might not. As they strolled down Regent Street towards Trafalgar Square, he was restlessly on the alert. All Wade's genial approaches at conversation were wasted on him. He did not intend to talk—even about the weather. One never knew these bulls from Scotland Yard.

It was in Cockspur Street that chance took a hand. A stout man, lumbering heavily in pursuit of an overloaded bus brushed blindly into the detective-sergeant. Wade staggered back and his grip on his prisoner loosened. In an instant Jim had wrenched himself free, while the detective measured his length on the pavement.

So far as Knuckleduster was concerned, it was fortunate that an empty taxi-cab should glide slowly by at that moment. He pulled open the door and stood on the running-board for a second while he addressed the driver.

"Chancery Lane," he said, "and rush it."

Satisfied that his injunction was being obeyed he slipped inside and flung himself upon the cushions with a grin. Circumstances had fallen his way and having a large stock of human nature, Knuckleduster was inclined to take the credit to himself. At any rate he had gained full advantage from them. It was not every man who could escape from custody in broad daylight in a frequented street with the daring and cleanness that he had shown.

His self-congratulation might have been less undiluted had he known that another taxi-cab containing four men was rolling along not fifty yards behind him. Further back still, Wade and the fat man who had been the original cause of the contretemps were walking amicably together towards Scotland Yard.

"As good as a picture-show," declared the fat man. "You've missed your vocation, Wade. You ought to be on the stage."

"I reckon Knuckleduster is riding away now and hugging himself at his own cleverness," said Wade. "Well, we've got several ends to work on now—things ought to be coming our way pretty soon."

Meanwhile as Knuckleduster fondly imagined, he was being carried farther and farther away from the instruments of justice. The luck that had sent the cab along just at the precise psychological moment never occurred to him as odd. Yet he was no fool. He knew that the chances were that Wade had had time after his recovery to take the number of the cab. In any event, taxi-cabs were always easily traced.

That was why he had given Chancery Lane as a direction in which to drive. Chancery Lane could afford no hint to those who followed up his trail. Within easy walking distance of that thoroughfare there were tubes, omnibuses, and trams to every part of London. It would be odd if, in the circumstances, he couldn't make a clean get-away. Yet he overlooked one fact—a fact which came as a shock to him when he realized it. He had no money. Every article of value he had on him had been taken when he was searched at Grape Street.

Knuckleduster cursed fluently as he thrust his hands hastily through his pockets with a faint hope that something might have been overlooked. It was vain.

In ordinary circumstances the prospect of trouble with a bilked taxi-driver would have weighed little on his mind. Now, however, he could not afford to have an altercation, which might end in the intervention of the police.

The cab slowed up at a slight block in the traffic and Knuckleduster cautiously unlatched the door. Standing on the running-board, he watched his opportunity and dropped off in the roadway somewhere near the Law Courts. Then he took to his heels in the direction of Kingsway where he plunged off to the right. Meanwhile, four men in the other taxi were gliding behind in easy pursuit. Not till he slowed to a walk did the cab stop to let two men emerge, who sauntered in the same general direction while the cab itself kept well in the background.

Knuckleduster had got away—at the end of a piece of string.

In twenty minutes' easy walking he came to, one of those severe Victorian by-streets of Bloomsbury, lined with the tall, ugly basement houses so familiar to the Bloomsbury boarder. He ascended the half-dozen steps to the front door and pressed the bell three times. The door opened without any obvious person behind it and Knuckleduster passed within.

Outside a couple of men strolled casually by and at the top of the street a taxi, obeying some unobtrusive signal, halted and Chief Detective-Inspector Garfield and Jimmie Silverdale descended.

XIX

THERE arrive moments when a Criminal Investigation Department man has to take chances; if possible, however, he prefers as a general rule to act on certainties. Cello Street, Bloomsbury—that is not its real name—was a short street containing at the most fifty or sixty houses of which No. 15, the house which Knuckleduster had entered, was roughly the center.

Once those two men had strolled by No. 15, Garfield took no further chances of alarming his quarry till he was good and ready. A couple of men picketed one end of the street. At the other end a taxi-driver was tinkering away with some machinery in the bonnet of his car. In the car, idly enjoying a cigarette sat Jimmie Silverdale. Garfield had disappeared in search of a telephone and presently returned, humming a comic song.

"If I'm right in the guess I'm making, Jimmie, this may be an amusing night."

Silverdale lifted his shoulders. "Always a chance of its being a wild-goose chase. This pigeon of yours—Knuckleduster Jim—may not be with Eston at all. He may be putting up at an ordinary boarding-house."

"That's conceivable, Jimmie, but"—Garfield carefully tapped out his pipe on the heel of his shoe—"but not very likely. You see I know Cello Street—and I know Knuckleduster. I wouldn't be at all surprised at anything Eston did but Knuckleduster has his limitations. That's probably why Eston is using him. And if I'm not away off my guess, I'll tell you another thing. Three or perhaps four of these austere old-fashioned houses are fitted up as gambling hells—perhaps something worse. Eston's adroit—I'll give him his due. At certain times there is probably a very keen lookout about here for any persons who look as if they were contemplating a police raid. I'm prepared to bet there's a bolt hole round one of these back streets and I want to stop it before we get busy. I've 'phoned through to Wade to bring half a dozen men."

With the arrival of his reenforcements, Garfield was able to direct a quiet investigation of the neighboring streets. The bolt hole he suspected he found in a narrow alley, giving access to the back entrances of Cello Street. There he posted three men. Having thus inspected the enemies' quarters, he held a little council of war with Silverdale and Wade, well out of sight of the place that was being kept, as the technical phrase goes, "under observation." Indeed to the casual passer-by there was no indication that anything unusual was stirring, or about to stir, the neighborhood.

An hour passed. Now and again a man or woman would enter the watched house. Two people had come from it, and once out of sight of the place, they had been stopped and questioned. Both adopted the same attitude of haughty resentment that collapsed like a pile of bricks when they realized that bluffing was no good.

"Look here," said Garfield. "You have been frequenting a gaming-house. That is illegal and, as a police officer, one should have a perfect right to arrest you. That is a course I am not anxious to take if you are reasonable. I'm not going to run any risks of a hint getting back that we are on the job. If you're willing to go to the nearest police station with one of my men and wait there for an hour, you'll hear no more of this. I take it you are anxious to avoid publicity. Now what do you say?"

In each case, they said "yes." More, a little adroit questioning revealed several things that it was good to know. As a result, Jimmie found himself deputed to make a reconnaissance of the house itself.

"I'd go myself," said Garfield, "but it's too much of a chance that someone will know me. And we mustn't let Knuckleduster catch sight of Wade. Here—" he drew a police whistle from his trousers pocket, "take this and you can bet we'll come a-running if we're needed. But we want to do the business quietly and neatly, if we can. I hate to make a fuss. You'll have to take your chance of Eston. Here's a card if you need one. It's always useful to have a spare card."

There was no immediate answer to Jimmie's ring at the door of No. 15. He stepped inside as the door, actuated by some unseen mechanism, glided open and immediately shut again as he crossed the threshold. He was in a dimly lighted hall, shoddily furnished—just such a hall as one might have expected from the exterior aspect of the house, save that three or four yards along, the passage was blocked by another door. He had an uncanny sense that, although he saw no one, he was being scrutinized and in a little the other door opened. A middle-aged man in well-fitting evening dress appeared.

"Did you want anyone, sir?" he demanded.

"Well," drawled Jimmie with well-assumed nonchalance, carrying out the instructions he had received from the people bagged by Garfield, "they do tell me that Mr. Smith lives here—Mr. Jones sent me." He presented the card Garfield had given him and the other took it between the tips of his fingers.

"Ah, yes. Captain Iles. Delighted to see you, captain. Won't you come in? It's a little early yet, and we haven't many people here but perhaps you'll take some refreshments."

The interior apartment to which Silverdale introduced was in great contrast to the hall. Two rooms had apparently been thrown into one and decorated and furnished with lavish disregard of cost. A heavy carpet on which every sound was deadened covered the floor and the walls were paneled in rich mahogany. Palms, big arm-chairs, and little occasional tables gave it something the appearance of a lounge, of an expensive club, and the center of the room was occupied by a table, now surrounded by a group of people who were intently watching the spin of a roulette wheel.

"Zero," announced the croupier and a hum of conversation broke out among the punters as the bank raked their money in. "Make your game, ladies and gentlemen."

In a swift glance, Silverdale failed to recognize anyone. His new acquaintance led him towards a small service bar and ordered drinks. "Here's to our better acquaintance, captain. I haven't seen you here before but I trust you'll be along now and again. What are you going to play? There's roulette, you see, and we have baccarat upstairs. Or, letting you into a secret, a few of us have a little room of our own upstairs where we play poker—just a select game, you understand. Of course, we have to be very careful and our clients are always cautious in their introductions. By the way, you gave the formula but you didn't say who really sent you."

Silverdale finished his drink. Here was a danger he' had hoped to avoid. There was, however, no help for it. He must face the situation.

"That's funny," he declared. "A chap at the club put me on to this. I know him as well as I know my own brother but for the life of me I can't remember his name."

"What club?"

Jimmie named one of the most exclusive clubs in London—a club that appeared on the card Garfield had lent him and the other nodded, apparently satisfied. "It would be Colonel Slaron, I expect—yes, that's probably who it is. He's a member of that show."

"He was a colonel, I believe," admitted Jimmie, dismissing the point. "If you don't mind, I'll just wander round for a little and watch things. I don't quite know what I'll fall for yet. I just slipped in on the spur of the moment. "

"Make yourself at home," urged his new friend, and left him.

Jimmie obeyed the injunction as literally as possible. In such a place as he judged this to be, a few pounds would not go far and he only had ten in his pocket. He staked two ten-shilling notes on roulette and lost. A gambler by instinct, he yet refrained from risking more at that moment. He could not tell how long it would be necessary to remain in the place and it was as well to have some money in reserve.

He wandered around the place, keenly alert to every detail. If Garfield was right, Hilary Sloane was somewhere in the building and he wanted to see her if possible.

For a little he sat in at baccarat. Playing as light as possible, he found luck with him. In the course of half an hour, his capital had turned into fifty pounds. Then the luck changed. He lost ten and rose.

No one paid any attention to him, as, hands in pockets, he sauntered apparently intently interested in the pictures which were displayed on most of the walls. Whenever he came to a door, he tried it but invariably those leading to the private portion of the house were locked. He had made up his mind to return and let the detective ransack the place by force when a big white panel in the ante-room of the saloon where baccarat was being played swung outwards and a woman emerged. Silverdale shrank behind a statue of Mercury and held his breath. It was Nora Dring.

She did not observe him and passed downstairs with quiet self-possession. The moment she was out of sight, Silverdale was at the panel, his fingers searching for the spring he knew must control it. He found it at last and slipped through, closing the panel behind him. A small flight of stairs led upwards and Jimmie followed them.

A woman passing along the corridor caught a glimpse of him, gave a gasp and came to a halt.

"Jimmie! Jimmie!" she whispered.

Regardless of the need for caution, he sprang up the remaining stairs three at a time with outstretched arms. All he knew was that Hilary Sloane was waiting for him.

Before he reached her, however, he recoiled. A blue-tinted barrel was behind the girl and behind that the lean, sardonic face of Eston.

"Good-evening, Mr. Silverdale," he said. "I told you we should meet again."

XX

To face the business end of an automatic was no new thing to Jimmie Silverdale. Yet four years of war, so far from making him careless, had given him a keen appreciation of the potentialities of a deadly weapon in the hands of a determined man. A reckless man might be brave; but he was usually a fool. There were men who could have borne tribute to Jimmie's courage; and these same men could also have told that he was far from being a fool.

He stood stock still and a slow grin spread over his face.

"Why, it's my dear old friend, Eston!" he exclaimed.

Eston advanced a step and with his left hand thrust Hilary behind him. He held his pistol very steadily. "Just myself, Mr. Silverdale," he said softly. "You expected to see me, of course—but not at this precise moment. Keep very still, please. I fancy you were trying to edge along a trifle and I prefer to have you at a reasonable distance. I'm a little at tension myself and something might happen if you moved. I suppose you are, so to speak, an advance courier for the Scotland Yard folk."

Jimmie yawned. "Dear old lad," he drawled. "Still playing lead for the pictures. For an intelligent man, Eston, you make me tired. You know as well as I do that you daren't murder me. It isn't done, old boy. Put down that howitzer and take things reasonably. In about an hour's time, when you're sitting comfortably in a nice, cool cell and are able to think things over, you will realize that this is good advice. You're hooked, old bean."

There was a sneer on Eston's face. "All very humorous, I've no doubt," he said. "I've never been a funny man myself and I'm not at all alarmed, thank you. I know that Knuckleduster didn't make a get-away to-night through his own brains. It was a frame-up, as I guessed. I've been expecting you and your friends for some considerable time."

"Well, I'm here," said Silverdale coolly.

"Yes, you're here. I think you'll stop here, too. I've made arrangements for just such a contingency. I'm afraid the *Daily Wire* will soon be missing one live, very alert, reporter. You see—"

Hilary suddenly gave a cry and sprang forward. "Look out, Jimmie!"

She was too late. From behind, two men had stealthily approached while the journalist was being held in conversation and, taken from behind, he stood not a dog's chance. In a few seconds he was lying prone, a heavy knee pressed into the small of his back and strong arms wrenching his wrists back till they could be lashed behind him.

At the same moment, Hilary had tried to spring past Eston to Jimmie's aid. The crook over-balanced and half fell but recovered himself. He seized the girl roughly by the wrists and hurled her backwards.

"You keep out of this, my lady," he ordered.

She picked herself up as the men jerked Jimmie to his feet. The journalist was very white. "You—Eston!" he snarled. "I'll find a way to get even with you for this!"

Eston knew that it was not his own predicament that had transformed Silverdale's jaunty nonchalance to white-hot passion, and an unpleasant smile passed across his features. "The dear lad," he smirked repeating Silverdale's words. "He is a chivalrous boy. He doesn't like to see the pretty dear knocked about. Don't you worry, Silverdale. Hilary and I understand one another. If I've hurt her, a kiss will put it right." He stepped back, placed his arm round the girl's waist, and bent his evil face to hers. "Won't it, Hilary?"

Tied though he was, it took the united strength of his two assailants to hold Jimmie Silverdale back then. Hilary, however, fought herself free and, with surprising vigor, crashed her fist full in Eston's face. He loosed her with an ugly oath and she fled along the corridor.

Eston wiped his face with a silk handkerchief and shrugged his shoulders. He seemed to have regained control of himself.

"A bit of a spitfire, Silverdale," he observed, "but I like 'em with a little spice. Now we'll have to deal with you. I'm afraid I cannot offer you that nice, cool cell which you kindly spoke about to me just now. But we'll try the next best thing—a little attic that we have fortunately got available as a spare room. I think perhaps that it might be advisable if you were gagged. I don't want to seem hard, but we never know what may happen."

Someone whipped a handkerchief over Jimmie's mouth and then with an escort on each side he was urged along. Eston led the way to what Jimmie judged was the top-most floor of the house and he was pushed into a tiny, bare, windowless room with, as he noticed almost automatically, a strong, heavy oaken door.

"I guess you will wait for your friends here," said Eston mildly—"that is, if they ever come. Just take a turn round his ankles, Jim, if you don't mind. We'll be on the safe side."

Lashed hand and foot, Jimmie heard the door closed, and the thrusting of the bolts and a clash as the key turned, told him that Eston was taking no chances.

To Jimmie Silverdale, tied hand and foot in that garret, things became curiously quiet. His ears strained to catch the slightest sound, he could hear nothing. Either the house was very substantially built or the people in it had become very noiseless.

Apart from the physical discomfort of his bonds, and the hard floor, the journalist was little worried. It could only be a matter of minutes at the longest before Garfield moved. If only he could have smoked a cigarette, he could possess his soul in patience. It was no use worrying over spilt milk.

Time passed very slowly. He wished he could look at

his watch. The floor became intolerably hard and he rolled over on his other side for a rest. His wrists and his ankles were sore and he had more than once felt a twinge of cramp. Something must have gone wrong—yet what could have gone wrong? Why had not the police carried out their raid? It must have been an hour—no, more likely two hours—since he had got into this place. He concentrated on an attempt to free his wrists. But there had been no mistake when they had been secured. The only result was an increased rawness of the skin.

Then he caught a slight sound and his eyes lighted. Muffled steps were ascending the stairs. Jimmie waited alert.

Bolts clicked back into place and, with the turning of the key, Eston slipped quietly into the room. He wore a hat and overcoat and seemed cool and smiling. He carried a candle.

"Well, Silverdale," he said, "I seem to have trumped your trick for once. You have had a little time for reflection. Don't you think you would be a wise man to call quits—you can get all you want if you come in with me. Ah, I forgot." He stooped and freed the bound man from his gag. "Now that's better. What do you think?"

Silverdale took one or two heavy breaths. The gag had oppressed him. "I'd be able to think better if you cut my hands and feet free," he observed.

Eston shook his head smilingly. "I have no doubt," he retorted. "You'll forgive me if I remark that I have a great respect for your physical prowess. Until we come to some amicable arrangement, I don't wish to put you in the way of temptation. You can talk quite well as you are."

"I don't know that I want to talk to you," said Jimmie. "You know that everything you say will be used as evidence against you at your trial."

The smile on Eston's face widened to an appreciative grin. "A sense of humor must be a great asset to a journalist. There are several reasons why what I say will not be used against me at my trial. For one thing I shall never be tried. Alternatively, as the lawyers say, you will not give evidence. Get that? We've got to come to a thorough understanding right now. Either you play partners with us, or the game ceases to interest you at all. You're right up against it."

"Really, this sounds interesting. You're going to murder me."

"Oh, dear, no I Nothing nearly so crude as that. You must give me some credit for a little ingenuity, my dear Silverdale. It may happen that, in a little while your friends outside—whom I have provided with occupation for a time—will take it into their heads to raid this place. As a fact, they'll have to break the door down to do it, and meanwhile there is enough petrol and enough matches in the place to make quite a considerable blaze. In the confusion, it is not unlikely that you will be overlooked. I'm afraid you are liable to get somewhat—ah—scorched, unless you listen to reason."

"Don't bluff."

Eston lifted his shoulders. "I was afraid you might think that. Therefore—I am going to tell you a few things—things that I'd only tell to a trusted ally—or a man who will be dead in a few hours."

The picture of scornful incredulity outwardly, Silverdale gave an inward shudder. He knew enough of Eston to realize that he was a man utterly without scruple, especially when pushed into a corner. Trapped and surrounded as he was, it was likely that he would go to any lengths to gain a chance. He believed that Eston was speaking the truth when he said he had found some method to distract the detectives. Otherwise, he would merely be wasting time with his prisoner.

"There were between twenty and thirty people in all in this place a little while ago," went on Eston. "They are mostly inoffensive fools with a taste for gambling which I try to gratify. You will probably have surmised that this place is mine, though as a rule I take no personal part in its management. Well, I've given them and the staff orders to clear out in different directions. I judge there isn't an enormous force of police in the cordon round about and they'll be reluctant to let anyone get away from here—as I say, their hands will be pretty full. I hate to break faith with my clients but after all it's only a question of a fine.

"Now I'm going to confess that I played a little trick on you when we bottled you on the stairs just now. I wanted to find out whether you were really in love with Hilary—or whether you were playing a devil of a deep game—or whether you knew, in fact, what I know. You fell for it. You are in love with the girl. What's more, she is in love with you."

"One of these days," observed Silverdale, "if you escape the hangman—which I doubt—someone will confer a benefit on society by strangling you. I'd volunteer for the job myself."

"Don't be hasty. I want you to hear me through, in patience. You are aware, of course, that the lady is not Miss Hilary Sloane at all. That she is a widow!"

A flicker of surprise passed across Jimmie's face to be instantly suppressed. He remembered his conversation with Garfield. He was determined to let Eston go as far as he would.

"I have known Miss Sloane some considerable time," he said. "I suppose it's waste of breath calling you a liar?"

"Ah, you are a little astonished. There is no reason why I should lie to you. I want your help and I am treating you quite frankly. The lady was secretly married some years ago in America, and she is the widow of our late lamented friend Harold Saxon. More than that—" he stretched out a hand eagerly—"she is his heiress. Oh, you may laugh, but I assure yon that I have my facts all straight. I have even a copy of the marriage certificate and I know that Saxon left the whole of his property to his wife."

"That latter point," said Jimmie, "explains why Velvet committed a burglary at Saxon's flat a few days before the murder took place."

"Draw what inferences you like," said Eston. "I am just telling you. Saxon's fortune, I may say, amounts to several millions—a stake worth playing for. I'm no piker. If you come in on this, you're a made man."

Silverdale puckered his brow, as one who considered a proposition. "If all this is true," he said, "and not a fantastic nightmare, where do I come in? I can see something of what you're after, but I don't see where I fit into the scheme. You're not making me this offer out of sheer altruism, I suppose?"

"Scarcely," said Eston dryly. "Listen. I have had this in mind for a year or more, ever since I learned that Saxon had made a secret marriage. First of all I had to find out where the girl was and chance helped me there since she was living with a lady who was under some obligation to me."

"Nora Dring?"

"That doesn't matter. What does matter is that I found her. I don't want to wear any halo with you and I'll admit if you like that I have made rather a specialty of using my knowledge of little family secrets now and again."

"Don't trouble about the gloss," said Silverdale. "Use the word 'blackmail.' It's shorter."

"As you like. I saw further than blackmail, though. Blackmail meant at the best a few thousands now and again. As I said before, I'm no piker. I believe in big business. If Saxon died, his widow would get his money. I took precautions to be sure of that. My idea was that I might marry the lady and so get my fingers on things. I believe I might have carried out that part of the program, had there not been complications—in other words yourself."

"You flatter me. As I understand it, what you intended to do was to kill Saxon and marry his widow?"

"If I had killed Saxon," said Eston, "I shouldn't have made the mistake of making it an obvious murder. That was clumsily done. Otherwise you have summed up the situation. I took advantage of things. If you had been less in Hilary's mind, it might have come off, or I might do what I shall do if you refuse my terms now and make her marry me whatever her feelings in the matter. Now, here is my offer. You want to marry her; she wants to marry you. I want to finger some of Saxon's money. You will take a million and I will take the rest."

"And what about the police?"

A sneer passed across Eston's face. "Oh, the police! You and I ought to be able to fix things so far as they are concerned. I'm not worried about that. They suspect Hilary of the murder but we'll be able to arrange an alibi."

"They don't suspect Hilary, as you know quite well. For one thing, she could never inherit Saxon's fortune if she had killed him."

"Well?" Eston shrugged his shoulders. "It doesn't matter whom they suspect. I'll give you my word that we'll be all right. Now, time is getting short. I've put my proposition up to you, what do you think of it?"

Silverdale struggled to a sitting position. "I think you have made a mistake. I'll see you in the deepest corner of the infernal regions before I agree to anything you put up. Go away."

"You're a little overstrained. Just consider it sanely for a moment. I offer you a million pounds more than you are fighting for. You only want the girl. Why refuse? You'll have nothing on your conscience. Look here, Silverdale, I'm in love with Hilary myself. On my soul, I shall be almost glad if you refuse."

Silverdale rolled over so that his back was towards the other and remained contemptuously silent.

"You've had your chance," said Eston. "I'll be damned if I'll waste more time with you!"

The door closed behind him.

XXI

So far as Garfield and the other Criminal Investigation Department men who were watching the place were concerned, Eston had estimated the situation well when he had turned loose a score of people for them to deal with. The Chief Inspector had too great a respect for the capacity of his antagonist to do anything hastily or to jump to any assumptions.

Among the scattered crew emerging from the house might be Eston himself. He had had experience of the crook's histrionic ability. Therefore he played safety. Men and women alike were questioned, scrutinized, and, despite their protests, hurried off to the nearest police station. The provision of escorts woefully skeletonized Garfield's meager force, but he calculated that he could well afford to wait. There were just enough men to watch the place but not enough to raid it. No one puts a ferret in a rabbit-hole, until the bolt holes are safely watched.

The inspector was, perhaps, a little concerned about Silverdale whose continued absence without giving the signal was, to say the least of it, disconcerting. For the time, however, Jimmie must look after himself. Garfield was not going to lose his quarry by pouncing too hastily. One by one his men trickled back to their posts, accompanied by other detectives from the divisional staffs of local police stations. Garfield took a turn up Cello Street keenly alert to discover any signs behind the closely curtained windows of the gambling house. There was nothing. From outside, at least, the place was dead. Garfield returned to his post at the corner.

"I'll not wait any longer for Silverdale," he told Wade. "We'll make a move. You take some men and try the back street."

Accompanied by the divisional detective inspector of
the district and a couple of other officers, he passed
quickly back along the street and mounted the steps of
the house. The signal that had secured Silverdale's
admission produced no reply. Garfield had scarcely
expected that it would. The wholesale migration of staff
and of patrons of the gambling house had been clear proof
that the inmates had taken alarm. Nevertheless,
formalities had to be complied with. Garfield thundered
with the knocker and gave repeated rings. Then he lifted
his heavily shod foot and kicked at the solid door.

"Look!" said the divisional man suddenly and Garfield
stepped back to follow the finger that pointed upwards. A
thin trickle of smoke was emerging from an open second-
floor window. Garfield ripped out a swear word. He
realized instantly that Eston had frustrated him again.
Criminals of that type will fight against heavy odds but
they do not willingly die in the last ditch. If Eston had
fired the house, he had done so not to die in its ashes but
to cover his retreat.

One of the detectives without waiting for orders was
already running full pelt down the road towards a fire
alarm. Another had climbed the railings and clinging like
a fly to what in similar houses in the neighborhood would
have been the dining-room window, protected his hand
with a cap and smashing a pane, inserted his arm and
pulled back the fastening. A wave of thick, black smoke
gushed out and, choking and gasping, he leapt clear.

"Smoke bombs," observed one of the other men.

Garfield slipped his arm through that of the divisional
detective inspector and pulled him back into the street.

"You take charge here," he said. "I've got half an idea
and I'm going to chance it."

It had been a matter of seconds since the alarm was
given, but already the street, which had seemed asleep up
to now, save for the detectives, was waking up. Heads
were appearing at windows and half-dressed figures at
open doors.

Garfield accosted a pajama-clad man two doors away. "Who's the owner or agent for this property?" he demanded, and as the man gave him the information he desired, he capped his question by another. "Where's the nearest telephone?" He accepted it as an interposition of Providence that there was one in that very house and expressing a word of thanks, he was soon feverishly turning over the leaves of a telephone directory.

Meanwhile, Jimmie Silverdale lay wondering what was going to happen. Since Eston had left him for the second time, the silence that had bothered him before had not been quite so obvious. There were muffled noises which he could not always interpret. Presently a smell of burning came to him.

Jimmie Sliverdale was a brave man but a shiver shook him from head to foot. Eston was carrying out his threat, then.

It is given to few people to face the slow approach of inevitable and painful death with stoicism. Jimmie was no stoic. He wrenched frenziedly at his bonds until his heart felt that it would burst but still the bonds held. By some inadvertence Eston had omitted to replace the gag and Jimmie raised his voice in loud, but what he instinctively knew, must be futile cries. If he could only have met his fate fighting, he would have been happier. But to die like this—roasted to death—appalled him. For the time, he was a trapped, unreasoning, frantic animal.

He called wildly on Eston, cursing him like a madman. Once or twice he found himself imploring Hilary to come and save him. Then exhaustion brought him back to sanity. He regained something of that philosophy which every man who has served in the trenches knows. A bullet either had one's name on it or it didn't. If he was going to be saved, he was going to be saved. If not—well, he would die in possession of his own self-respect, not as a screaming coward. He set his lips grimly.

The smoke was increasing now and eddying in under

the crack of the door. He began to cough. He regretted now that the gag had been removed. It would at least have protected him to some extent from this blinding, choking torment. He rolled over and tried to hold his mouth and nostrils close to the bare boards. It was a feeble expedient but it failed in its purpose.

His nerves were beginning to fail him. He saw visions. There were people around him—people who were slipping a knife under the cords that held him. There were voices—dim, far-away voices calling him. Why couldn't they let him alone? He was just going to drop into a pleasant doze—and now!

Backing pains affected the muscles of his limbs and brought back his fleeting senses.

"Oh, Jimmie, Jimmie! If you don't pull yourself together, what shall I do?"

He sat up, shakily. The room was full of swirling wreaths of heavy smoke. Dimly in the darkness, he made out a figure, gaunt and spectral, with something round its head that gave it a singularly weird and fantastic effect. The figure was kneeling near him with one arm round his shoulders. He sensed, rather than recognized, her identity.

"Hilary!" he gasped.

"Yes, it is Hilary. Can you stand, Jimmie? Here—let me wind this round your head." She twisted something round his face so that the intolerable smoke pangs were minimized. "Now, don't talk. Try to stand."

Hilary Sloane was a good type of the modern athletic girl. She did not believe that femininity implied weakness and she had need of all her strength now, for Jimmie was as weak as a kitten. Half-supporting, half-carrying him, she groped her way towards the door. At the stairs, he stumbled and only a superhuman ef- fort on her part saved them both from disaster. Smoke was rolling up from below in thick, oily wreaths, with weird effects, as in the far distance little flashes of blue and yellow flame appeared.

Staggering, choking, gasping, they descended the stairs, a feat only to be achieved with infinite slowness. As they neared the ground-floor, the heat became more intense and the smoke hung more closely. Jimmie swayed and would have fallen but for the pressure of that slim arm against him.

"Hold up! Oh, Jimmie, hold up! Only a few steps more and we shall be safe."

He felt that they were passing into the basement and the air grew a trifle clearer. She stooped and fumbled on the ground until she felt a ring-bolt and flung back a trapdoor. Then came her supreme task. A steep ladder led to the depths. It was out of the question that they could descend side by side, as they had down the stairs. It was clear that Jimmie could not make the trip unaided, and though he was a comparatively lightly built man, Hilary doubted if she was equal to the task of carrying him down. The dilemma, however, had to be solved. There was no time for hesitation.

"You must slide down, Jimmie," she urged. "Understand?" She shook him slightly, as if that would make her meaning clear. "You will probably bruise yourself but that cannot be helped. It is better than remaining here."

"I'll try, Hilary," he gasped.

She supported him to the opening, and getting a firm grip of his collar, let him down till she could bear the strain no longer. Then she let go and he slid to a heap at the bottom of the ladder. Hilary followed, closing the trapdoor behind her. They were in a cellar as dark as a pit but comparatively free from the suffocation and heat of the house itself. Silverdale had fainted in good earnest.

When he came to, feeling very weak and sore, they were still in impenetrable darkness. He felt his own hand clasped in a soft, warm one and heard the sound of gentle sobs. Hilary—the girl who had no nerves—was crying. She ceased instantly as she felt the pressure of her hand returned.

"Are you all right, old boy?"

"Fit as a fiddle, dear," he lied brazenly, though he ached all over and felt as weak as a rat. "What are you crying for?"

"I wasn't crying," she declared indignantly. "At least—Jimmie—I suppose I was a bit overdone."

He sat up. "I don't wonder at that. You've been through more than most men could stand. Where are we?"

She struck a match and by its glimmer, he saw that they were in a small, low-pitched bricked tunnel, the damp oozing from the walls. "I don't know exactly," she admitted. "This is the secret way out, according to Eston, but where it leads to, I haven't the faintest idea."

Silverdale was a man who possessed wonderful powers of recuperation. He felt his strength returning to him with every breath he took and he remembered with a shudder the nightmare horror they had passed through. He retained only a shadowy notion of what had happened since he had lain in that garret, waiting for death.

"It occurs to me, Hilary," he said, "that you have saved my life."

She smoothed his face with her free hand. "Don't be silly, Jimmie," she said.

"It's true," he insisted. "I'd be a pretty cheap sort of a corpse just now if it hadn't been for you. I'm afraid my legs are a bit wobbly yet, so if you don't mind we'll wait a bit before we begin to explore this private tunnel of Mr. Eston's. Meanwhile, you might tell me how it all happened."

She laughed—a merry, musical, happy laugh, that echoed strangely among their dismal surroundings. "You got my note?" she asked.

"The note you left on the house-boat—sure!"

"And you don't think that I murdered Sir Harold Saxon now?"

He lifted the hand that was clasped in his own to his lips. "That's your answer," he said. "Now, how did you get away from Eston?"

"Oh, there was nothing in that. He knew a great deal and guessed more after you and he met on the stairs. He told us—Nora and myself—that the place was surrounded and that we had a back way out through which he proposed to take us if the police tried to force an entrance. 'A private emergency exit'—he described it. I asked what he had done about you. He laughed—he can be diabolical at times, you know, Jimmie—and said that he had you safely stowed away in a lumber room. 'He's a bright lad,' he said, 'and I take rather a paternal interest in him. Since you won't marry me, I thought that it wouldn't be a bad plan to elect him to the office of bridegroom. What do you think'?"

She fell silent and Jimmie, though he couldn't see her face, knew that she was blushing. "Very kind of Mr. Eston," he said dryly. "Go on, Hilary."

"Well, after that, he went away. Of course I didn't know what to think, except that he had some black scheme at the back of his mind. Then he returned, told me that you had refused point-blank to marry me and that he had turned you loose, as he phrased it, to 'stew in your own juice.' We were hustled downstairs and through the trapdoor down here. I smelt the smoke and demanded to know what he had done with you. He protested that you were quite all right —that he had set you loose and that you would be able to take care of yourself. I knew that he was lying and though he had hold of my arm, I tore myself from him and dashed back and somehow got through the trapdoor in front of him. He followed me no farther though I could hear him swearing.

"The place was full of smoke. He had told me that they had used a combination of smoke-bombs and petrol. The smoke was meant to hold back the police till the place got well alight and so prevent them from discovering our retreat too soon. I tore my skirt off and bound a piece of it round my face. So at last I found you."

"I know men who have won the V.C. for less," said

Silverdale. "Now our immediate problem seems to be where are we and how do we get out? Eston seems to have wriggled out of his difficulties once again. Have you any matches?"

"I have got one left," said the girl.

"And I have none. Well, I should save yours in case we want it. Meanwhile, we'll grope our way along and see what happens."

He pulled himself stiffly to his feet and, arm in arm, they began to grope their way along the tunnel.

XXII

BIG business in crime as big business in ordinary commercial pursuits takes account of contingencies. Eston, when he became proprietor of a gambling hell, took account of the risks as well as the profits. It was to minimize these risks that he had had a tunnel constructed at an outlay which many people might have looked upon as prohibitive, but which he regarded as an insurance.

Although the possibility that he might find use for it personally may have been in his mind, it is doubtful if that was a prime reason. There are many people who frequent gambling houses who would hate the publicity of a police court. It was their convenience rather than his own that Eston had in mind when he provided this other unobtrusive exit.

The emergency which had now arisen, however, had thrown the question of preserving the "good-will" of his clients into the shade. In fact, Eston had flung them, as well as the permanent staff of the place, into the street, as part of the policy to occupy the police till he was ready. His chief concern was to get away whole to carry out his own greater plans.

When Hilary rushed back into the burning house he had pursued her to the trapdoor and then paused, baffled. He had nerve on occasions but he calculated swiftly and two things flashed across his mind. The likely probability was that the girl would be driven back by the flames and smoke, in which event he would be waiting to deal with her. Alternatively if she would be mad enough to fight her way to the top of the house, her chances of return were negligible. To follow her was to court certain death. Eston preferred to wait.

A couple of minutes had perhaps elapsed when Nora Dring, picking her way by the aid of an electric torch, returned. She laid a hand lightly on his arm.

"She has got away?" she asked.

He swore fiercely. "She slipped me. She's gone sheer crazy over the pen-pusher. I guess they're both burned to cinders—or will be. It's no good waiting. Where's Velvet and Jim?"

"They didn't stop."

"No, they wouldn't," he sneered. "You've got more nerve than either of them, my girl. Why did you come back?"

She slipped her hand through his arm and he could feel her trembling. "We were friends—Hilary and I," she said.

He laughed scornfully and quickened his pace.

"She was your friend, you mean," he corrected. "I hadn't noticed that you had been playing the Jonathan to her David stunt—not to any extent since I've known you. Why, girl—" he halted as though seized by a sudden inspiration, disengaged her arm and held her with his torch blazing full on her face—"if I'm not away out in my guess, you'll not be sorry that she's gone. You little devil—you're glad!"

Eston was not squeamish. He had done cruel things in his fight against society and he was brutally reckless of everything, even human life, when he had an end to achieve. He had left Jimmie Silverdale to a painful death without a pang of remorse, but there was a light in the girl's green eyes which stirred even in him a feeling of revulsion. She was shivering beneath the grip of his hand but there was a cold smile on her face.

"Perhaps—I'm not so sorry as I might have been," she confessed. "I liked Hilary—she was useful to me in the old days. But she became a prig—and I can't stand prigs."

He jerked his thumb backwards and regarded her cynically. "So you don't mind much that we've left her behind—there. By God! I hate to think of it—and you smile!"

"You see, you were in love with her—or thought you were," she countered. "No, I didn't come back because of Hilary. I came because of you."

"Of me?" Eston took no trouble to conceal his sneering surprise. "I didn't know you were interested in me to that extent."

She sprang forward suddenly and threw her arms around his neck. She was kissing him hotly, passionately, clinging convulsively to him in an ecstasy of passion. Eston pushed her brutally away.

"Ugh!" he gasped contemptuously, "you're mad!"

"*It was you,*" she insisted, speaking with a fierce intensity as she faced him. "Why have I been helping you all this while, blindly, unhesitatingly? If you hadn't been taken up so with Hilary, you would have seen. I'm the woman for you. I'm glad she's gone—glad, glad, glad!" She stamped her foot. " I have helped you but I tell you this—you would never have married her. I'd have killed you both first!"

"You would, eh?" he said quietly. "I'm almost inclined to believe you, my dear. Now, if you don't mind, we'll discuss the question at some more suitable time. Just now, the main idea seems to me to get away from here. You'll feel better when we reach the fresh air."

"Don't address me as if you were speaking to a child," she snapped. "I'm a woman and I'm not to be played with." Her tone changed and she sank on her knees in front of him, gripping his hand tightly. "Oh, my dear, my dear! Say that we shall—"

Eston cut her short. Even if he had had the inclination, he felt it was no time for such a scene. Hilary had attracted him; but Nora Dring, though she had proved useful in the game he was playing, had never caused his pulse to move a single beat quicker. If Hilary Sloane had gone, his use for her companion had vanished. He cared nothing for her sex or her feelings. He pulled his hand away and pushed her roughly aside. She fell with a little moan and he pressed on, unheeding.

"Get out of my way, you Jezebel!"

She picked herself up and followed him without a word and the darkness concealed her face. Nora Dring, it is probable, would have been ready to take many things from Eston. The physical violence with which he had repulsed her counted nothing; it was the contemptuous nonchalance with which he brushed her from his path that grated on her.

He was half a dozen steps or so in front of her when she called after him. "You had better listen to me."

"We can't hang about," he retorted and pushed on. The exit from the tunnel was almost the exact replica of the entrance, a low-pitched cellar from which one left by way of a ladder and trapdoor. It was as he approached the ladder that Eston's pace became slower. Some uncanny intuition warned him that all was not well and yet there was no obvious reason for the supposition. He paused with one foot on the ladder, extinguished his torch and listened. He could hear nothing.

Indeed, it may have been the extraordinary quietness of the house above that confirmed his latent suspicion. It was impossible that this means of retreat could have been guessed and yet—and yet!

He thrust a hand out behind him and whispered a warning to the girl. "H'st!"

Still the silence hung about them, oppressive, impenetrable as the darkness itself. Then someone sneezed. In an instant, Eston was back at the mouth of the tunnel, an automatic in his hand, the beam from his torch concentrated steadily on the trapdoor ladder. He raised his voice. "Is that you, Jim?" and the trapdoor swung back.

"Come right on, guv'nor," said a husky voice. "It's all quiet."

The hand that held the electric torch shook a little. Eston's senses were too keyed up for him to make a mistake. At another moment he might have taken that voice for Jim's—but not now. He knew that, somehow, in spite of all his foresight, he had been outwitted. He was trapped.

The realization of all it might mean swept across him in a flood. Not only had he lost the game—the big game for millions that he had been playing—but he had overreached himself. Whatever their suspicions in the Saxon business, they could prove little—certainly not, he told himself, that he had had any finger in the event that led to the murder of that eminent munitioneer.

This, however, was different. There was Jimmie Silverdale, for instance. He was known to be in the gambling house when it had been fired and there would be remains. No legal adroitness, no slice of luck could possibly save him from conviction on that charge of murder, once he fell into the hands of the police. He had blundered, execrably, horribly. He had played and lost.

Nora Dring crept close to him. "What is it?" she whispered.

He kept his eyes steadily on the shaft of light that flickered on the ladder and would outline the first figure to descend. "It's the gentlemen from Scotland Yard, if I don't miss my guess," he said. "We're in for it, my dear."

She glanced apprehensively towards the trapdoor. Then before he could guess her purpose, she had raised her voice. "Is Mr. Garfield there? It's Nora Dring speaking."

"Keep quiet, you!" ordered Eston sharply. Then he shrugged his shoulders. The situation, from his point of view, was as bad as it could be. There was nothing the girl could do that would worsen it. He raised his voice. "Don't trouble to answer, Garfield. You're a darned poor ninnie, and I've had you taped this last minute. You'll get cramp if you stick outside that trapdoor waiting for me to come up. You've got to come and fetch me."

Something white appeared in the opening of the trapdoor. The pressure of Eston's finger tightened and the explosion of the automatic in the confined space was deafening. Nora Dring gave a half-suppressed scream and the white face in the opening disappeared.

"Not so bad," came the cool voice of the chief detective inspector. "You've chipped a bit out of my ear, Eston. I'll forgive you that if you'll be the reasonable man I know you to be and come up without making a fool of yourself."

Eston hesitated. His arm curved slowly till the muzzle of the pistol was resting against his temple. His finger curled slowly round the trigger. That would be the quickest way. It was all just the same in the end. Why should he endure the long-drawn-out formalities of the law when—? The pressure of his finger relaxed and the weapon dropped to his side. After all, he was not taken yet. He would not take that way out until the last minute. There was no telling what might happen, desperate though the affair seemed.

"I hate to disappoint you, Garfield," he said sardonically. "You haven't got your hooks on me yet, but if you want to take tea with me, come along. We will be a merry party. You can sit on that trapdoor till it's red-hot and you can't find me walking into your arms."

He heard the striking of a match as Garfield lit his pipe. The inspector had learned more than he needed to know when he had placed his head inside the trapdoor. He was disposed to take things comfortably. "That's all right, then," he said amiably. "We've got all the time there is and we're ready to wait. You'd find yourself much more comfortable in our hands—but suit yourself. If Miss Dring likes to come up, we'll make her welcome. Is Miss Sloane there?"

"She is not," answered Eston, and composed himself to his vigil.

"Well, what does Miss Dring say?"

Nora Dring, her face white, her knees trembling, collapsed in a heap at Eston's feet. "I'll stay with Mr. Eston," she declared shakily.

XXIII

MR. JOSIAH GARFIELD smoked steadily and philosophically as he sat in a chair by the side of the open trapdoor. Two other men were with him, also smoking, and tied hand and foot in a remote corner of the kitchen lay Velvet Fred and Knuckleduster Jim. As the chief inspector had remarked, he had all the time there was and if the business was to resolve itself into a game of patience, he did not greatly mind.

Of what had happened at the burning gambling hell he had not the slightest idea. He was bent single-mindedly on securing Eston and he was very happy.

Some day, he reflected, he would tell of this exploit. There were angles of it that made him realize that he was a great man. It was a flash of genius that had made him think that a man of Eston 's caliber would not fire the place unless he had some secret and certain method of escape. He had argued that men who had made a life-profession of crime, as Eston had, do not commit suicide and he had proved himself right in this case, at least.

From that proposition, the idea of a tunnel had followed logically and there was only one reasonable probability—that it had its exit at some other house in the vicinity. So the detective had played his hunch. An inquiry of the estate agent had revealed the fact that a "Mr. H. Smith" had taken another house on agreement in a street fifty yards back at the same time that he had taken the place in Cello Street. And now Garfield was sitting by a trapdoor with Eston underneath and two or three men connected with the case actually in his hands. Yes, he felt very pleased.

His thoughts reverted to Silverdale. He had great belief that that young man would land right side up on his feet whatever happened, and yet he felt some uneasiness. It was curious that nothing had been seen or heard of him since he had entered the place. And Hilary Sloane. Why was she not down there with Eston? It might be that the crook was lying, but it was all mightily curious.

The entrance of Wade and two or three more men disturbed his reflections. The sergeant, his evening dress torn, his face smoke-grimed and dirty, his some-time snowy shirt-front blackened and soiled, glanced with a grin at the two men in the corner.

"I was told you were here, sir," he reported.

"Yes, I'm here," agreed Garfield. "How's it going? Any news of Silverdale?"

Wade shook his head gloomily. "The place is gutted," he said. "If he is in it, I'm afraid it's all up with him."

"H'm." Garfield took his pipe from his mouth. "That's a pity. I rather liked the lad. I'd hate to think that he'd gone under like that. However—" He lifted his massive shoulders.

Wade's gaze wandered to the open trapdoor and he lifted his eyebrows interrogatively.

"Yes, Eston is down there. He's got a gun and he made some uncommonly good practice when I tried to get a glint at him." He touched his injured ear, on which a slight clot of blood showed, tenderly. "He's not feeling very amiable just now is Mr. Eston." He raised his voice. "Are you there, Eston? What have you done with Silverdale?"

There was a chuckling laugh from below. "Ask me?" retorted Eston sarcastically. "He's out of the game."

The two detectives looked at each other and Garfield frowned. Both were sorry, but it was all in the day's work. Wade stooped to glance down the open trapdoor, but Garfield stopped him with a touch. "I wouldn't do that," he warned.

The sergeant heaved himself up and spat through the opening. "What are we going to do about that swine?" he said. "We're not going to leave him there to laugh at us.

I'm willing to chance it and go down and pull him out if you give the word."

Eston, to whom every word of the conversation was audible, laughed loudly.

"Come along!" he taunted.

The chief inspector shook his head. "No need to be in a hurry," he said. "We've got him safe enough. We put up a sweet little ambush, Wade. I'm sorry you weren't here to enjoy it. Jim and Fred there just walked into our arms. They were in such a hurry that they didn't know what had happened till it was all over. Here—" he addressed one of the detectives who were listening—"you slip down and get a taxi and then a couple of you can get 'em to Grape Street. Might as well get 'em cleared out of here."

The man addressed gave a jerk of the head to signify that he comprehended the order and vanished. Wade leaned over close to his chief and muttered something in a low voice.

The chief inspector listened thoughtfully. "There's a girl down there," he observed. "We might try to get her up." He raised his voice. "Miss Dring," he called.

"Yes." The answer floated up clearly but there was a slight tremor in the voice.

"I want to ask you to come up here and surrender yourself. You will be treated with every consideration, but if you refuse I can't answer for what may happen. I strongly advise you to do the sensible thing. We may find it necessary to use Mr. Eston's own methods and smoke him out."

"Surrender?" The girl's voice was still more tremulous. "I don't understand. Do you mean that you are going to arrest me?"

"Come up," said Garfield gently. "We will explain everything when you are up here." He paused. "Are you coming?"

The girl's voice as she answered was firm—firm with the accent of desperation. "If you are going to arrest me, I will not come. Will you give me your word that if I come up, I shall go free and unharmed, without any reservation!"

A wry smile showed on Garfield's face. "A pretty cool proposal," he muttered under his breath. Then, "I can give you no undertaking of any kind. You will be treated with courtesy and if you have nothing on your conscience, you have nothing to fear."

"I'll not come," she said decisively.

For a while nothing happened except the removal of the prisoners. Now that the burning house and its surroundings no longer needed such careful watching, Garfield had plenty of help at hand. To tell the truth he was becoming a little impatient. If Nora Dring had not been down below, he might have taken a chance and waited for a while. There were many reasons why he should and only one why he should not. There was just the chance that the girl might take the one way of escape that lay open to her. Garfield did not want a dead woman on his hands—he wanted a live prisoner.

Leaving the watching of the trapdoor to others, he and Wade retired to another room where they could lay their plans in privacy. Here they were joined by Rack, the divisional detective inspector from Grape Street, and the divisional detective inspector in charge of the Bloomsbury district.

It took a matter of rather less than five minutes to complete their very simple arrangements and they returned to the kitchen. Four big men, they walked very quietly and in silence grouped themselves round the opening of the trapdoor. Garfield stooped and suddenly swung his big body clear, gripping the edge of the opening and leaping clear of the ladder down into the cellar.

He swerved sideways as he landed in the darkness and flashed on an electric torch. He carried an automatic in his pocket but he had the ingrained reluctance of the London police to use a lethal weapon even in self-defense and even as Eston opened a reckless fusillade, he did not draw it.

One by one as in a game of follow-my-leader, his companions leapt through the opening, each flashing their torches in Eston's face. Dazzled and blinded, he fired wildly in their general direction but only one shot took effect and that through the fleshy part of Rack's arm.

Before the last man had touched the ground, Garfield was within a couple of yards of Eston. There was a swish of skirts as Nora fled back along the tunnel and the crook, after hesitating for a fraction of a second, turned and followed her, reloading his pistol as he ran. He outpaced the girl and as he passed her, she stumbled. The next moment Garfield had gone headlong over her.

As he rose a defiant shot echoed from ahead in the tunnel. He had his hand round the girl's wrist and felt a convulsive shudder shake her. "Oh," she moaned and dropped again.

"Are you hit?" asked the inspector but there was no reply. He turned his torch on her, reckless that he was making a mark that would show vividly in the tunnel, and his eyes told him the answer.

Some of the other men dropped down as the fusillade opened and were crawling along the tunnel. He felt a hand at his knee and heard Wade's voice. "It's no good, sir. He's got us cold. Now he's got a start, he can wipe us all out in this narrow passage if we try to rush him. We'd better go back."

"Can he?" said Garfield between his teeth. "Here's the girl. She's been hit. A couple of you take her back and see whether she's badly hurt."

They passed the girl back while bullets splintered on the brickwork around them. Wade had put the situation in a nutshell. It seemed hopeless to carry out the attempt at arrest any further. Eston had realized the strength of his position, and thoroughly reckless and desperate, was determined that nothing should dislodge him.

Very reluctantly Garfield stretched himself full length on the greasy floor of the tunnel and leveled his own weapon.

XXIV

To Hilary Sloane and Jimmie Silverdale, there came the sound of voices magnified and distorted by the echo of the tunnel. Silverdale had his arm round the girl's waist and his clasp tightened warningly. Some inkling of what had happened flashed across his mind and he whirled her about.

"I miss my guess if Garfield hasn't pulled off a trick this time," he whispered. "It looks to me as if Eston had left things a little too late."

She pressed closer to him and they stole backwards for half a dozen yards. Then they halted and, pressed close against the brick wall, listened tensely. Time moved on leaden wings but nothing happened, though now and again some slight shuffling of feet warned them there was someone in front of them. Then suddenly lights showed at the end of the tunnel and the sound of pistol shots magnified till they seemed like the reverberation of heavy artillery close at hand come down to them.

"That will be Eston—or some of his pals," muttered Jimmie. "The police wouldn't fire at all, except as a last resort."

There was a flash of feet and Silverdale pushed the girl behind him. Again revolver shots broke out and he crouched forward, somewhat in the attitude of a runner prepared for a start. Eston, backing slowly, was close at hand, and the journalist heard Garfield's voice as Nora Dring was hit. The detective's torch gave him a glimpse of figures farther up the tunnel. Then the torch went out and he jumped.

Any warning to the detectives must have also warned Eston. Silverdale knew and accepted the risk. As he leapt he heard a bullet shatter on the wall behind.

"Don't shoot—it's I—Silverdale!" he yelled.

His hands encountered something yielding and a numbing blow took him in the shoulder. The journalist's full strength had not yet come back to him and he reeled. It was Eston's opportunity but he never repeated the blow. All the demoniac fury of the past few minutes had left him and he cowered away with an inarticulate guttural sound.

Garfield, who had reached a conclusion with the first sound of Silverdale's voice, was on his feet in an instant. One of his assistants was behind him and switched on his torch. By its light they saw Silverdale and Eston swaying to and fro, the journalist shaking the other as a terrier shakes a rat. Eston had dropped his pistol and was offering no resistance. The chief inspector's hand descended on the crook's shoulder and he pushed Silverdale away with the other.

"That will do, Jimmie," he said quietly. "He's had enough."

Two or three torches were illumining the tunnel by this time. Garfield slipped a hand to Eston's wrist. Another big detective had him by the other arm. The crook shrugged his shoulders.

"I seem to have lost," he said, "but if I had known—"

Garfield cut him short. "You are under detention on suspicion of being concerned in the murder of Harold Saxon," he said hastily. "It is my duty to warn you that anything you say may be used in evidence. You've given us a hot run, Eston, but we've got you now."

A wry spasm of laughter shook the crook. "Good old square boots," he retorted. "You're barking up the wrong tree still. If I'd known what I know now, I'd have cut a loss and walked into your arms at the top of that trapdoor. You'll never be able to prove me guilty of that if you try for a million years."

Garfield nodded his head. "That's interesting. And yet you did your best to lay some of us out, rather than take the chance of being charged. Queer thing for an innocent man to do, wasn't it?"

Silverdale, who stood quietly by, regaining his breath, interposed. "I think I can explain that. Eston was afraid that he would be taken for murder and for that reason he put up a fight rather than take what was coming to him—but it was not the murder of Harold Saxon that he had in mind."

"Meaning?" interjected Garfield.

"Meaning that he thought I was burnt to a cinder by now. He hadn't reckoned on finding you at the other end of his emergency exit and it threw him out of his stride. If it hadn't been for Miss Sloane here, I shouldn't be giving you this exposition now."

"You're a clever lot of ginks, aren't you?" sneered Eston. "You know the dickens of a lot and all! Listen! I'll tell you something. I played the big game and I lost so it doesn't very much matter now. Silverdale is right in this, that I never was afraid of being arrested for the murder of Sir Harold Saxon, because I didn't do it. On that I am perfectly innocent. Until an hour ago, there was always a chance that I could handle the Saxon fortune while I had my hands on Saxon's widow. For some reason—" he glanced sideways at Hilary standing with her arm through Jimmie's in the semi-darkness behind the glow of the torches—"she would not fall in with my views. I gathered that Silverdale might succeed where I had failed and I put the proposition to him. In doing so, I had to reveal certain parts of my plan that it was advisable no man should know unless he was working with me. Silverdale refused and I had to make sure that he would tell no tales. I counted on getting clean away—" he shrugged his shoulders—"but I was mistaken. So with the knowledge there would be awkward inquiries after Silverdale, I put up a fight. There was all to be gained by fighting and nothing to be lost. When I heard Silverdale's voice out of the darkness, just now, I began to see it was hopeless. He knew the story."

"We'll move off now, if you don't mind," said Garfield without comment on the prisoner's statement.

Not until they were in the comparatively free air of the kitchen where Eston had laid his unsuccessful ambush did Garfield again address the prisoner who now stood in the custody of other detectives.

"I'm not entitled to say this to you, Eston, but I'm going to take a chance and relieve my mind. Whether you were the actual person who murdered Saxon or not, you organized that crime. For you to carry out your schemes, it was necessary that he should die. Don't ask us to believe that it was mere coincidence. It. suited your convenience, too well."

Eston's eyes glowed. "I dare say you've got a whole heap of evidence against me," he said sarcastically. "But you'll never hang me for murder."

Garfield stooped to pick up his pipe which lay where he had left it when he had leapt through the trapdoor.

"The pity of it all from your point of view, Eston," he observed, "is that you never realized you were off the rails. You laid your plans on a wrong foundation."

The crook eyed the inspector up and down suspiciously. "What are you trying to draw out of me now, I wonder," said he.

Garfield shook his head guilelessly. "Nothing," he replied. "I've got all I want against you. I shall be able to prove enough when yon go up for trial. I shall prove that you had Miss Dring under your influence and that it was through her that you came into association with Miss Hilary Sloane, whom you believed to be the wife of the man now dead. I can prove the movements of Knuckleduster Jim, Miss Dring, and yourself up to within an hour of the time the murder was committed. I can prove that the person who killed Sir Harold Saxon left you with that deliberate purpose."

Eston knew that he was being keenly watched. He realized that Garfield would not be wasting time in discussing the affair unless he' had some purpose. The crook had been trained in a cautious school and was well on his guard. His face was impassive while Garfield made his indictment.

"Bluff!" he commented scornfully. "Sheer bluff."

Garfield ignored the interruption. "I shall prove all this," he resumed, "but as I remarked just now, you went to a deal of trouble on a mistaken conception. You imagined you had identified Lady Saxon."

One of the detectives pulled forward a hard wooden chair and passed it to Eston. He sat down nonchalantly and crossed his legs. Two deep thoughtful lines appeared on his forehead and he watched Garfield intently.

"Why waste time?" he asked coldly. " This is a beautiful fairy-tale, isn't it?"

"Harold Saxon married a woman who called herself Hilary Sloane in America," went on the inspector. "The knowledge was a useful asset to a man in your profession, of course—particularly as Saxon was not living with his wife here. That was the assumption you acted on and it was a false one. Did it never occur to you, Eston, that the lady who married Saxon might not have used her own name for the ceremony—that in fact it was not Miss Sloane who was the bride?"

The point to which he had been leading up went home. There was no doubt about that. Eston leaned forward eagerly, forgetful that he was being watched, and his lean face was set in a scowl.

"What's that you say?" he demanded. "She is not Lady Saxon?" He pointed a slim finger at Hilary.

"That's what I said," agreed Garfield. "You've made a blunder, Eston."

Eston's lips moved but for a little there issued no sound from them. He saw no reason for doubting Garfield's word, although it was only a bare assertion. He was a man of imagination and it bit like acid into his mind that he had been tilting at windmills. He had erected his supreme edifice on foundations of sand, for if Hilary Sloane was not Lady Saxon, none of the risks he had taken were justified. He cursed his folly silently. A suspicion, hazy at first, but growing more definite as his

brain turned over the import of Garfield's words, grew in
his mind.

"If you are right," he said, "Lady Saxon is—"

"Miss Nora Dring," said Garfield.

A venomous curse came from Eston. "That red-haired
devil. She never said a word. If I had known—if I had
known—"

In a tumult of passion, he had forgotten where he
was. As he recalled the episodes of the past few days,
much that had been obscure or unnoticed, became plain
to him. It was bitter to reflect that the girl had flung
herself at his head and that he had repulsed her—she the
heiress to millions. And now—now it was too late.
Whatever else the police held against him, for one thing
alone he was certain of a long term of penal servitude—
the attempted murder of Jimmie Silverdale. He squared
his. shoulders.

"Garfield," he said, "I'm in for it. That girl has let me
in whether she meant to or not. I'm going to talk."

"You can make a voluntary statement if you wish,"
said Garfield, coldly indifferent but with a glow of
triumph inside.

"I'll do that," said Eston resolutely.

XXV

JOURNALISM is an exacting taskmaster. Worn as Silverdale was, reluctant as he was to leave Hilary, his first duty was to the newspaper that employed him. He held in his hands the biggest newspaper story of years and though the actual raid and the burning of the house in Cello Street had already brought down the battalions of Fleet Street, there was nothing that they could have gained that would in any way take the gloss off his big story.

So it was that leaving Hilary with Garfield, who promised that she should be carefully looked after, he hurried to Fleet Street.

It was late and the early editions of the paper had already been dispatched, but a number of the night staff, including the chief sub-editor to the news-editor, were still on duty. They welcomed the sunken-eyed Silverdale boisterously.

"You've been left standing this time, Jimmie. While you've been hunting will-o'-the-wisps, there's been a big stunt up in Bloomsbury—a great yarn and arrests wholesale. We've given it four columns."

Jimmie searched his pocket for the makings of a cigarette and rolled it languidly. "I know," he said. "I was there."

The news-editor had had a wearing night and his temper was a little jagged. "You were there," he repeated. "Then why the policemen didn't you let us hear from you? See here, Silverdale, you may think you're the big noise on this sheet, but you've got no right to hold things up till the paper's gone to press. Why didn't you 'phone"

Silverdale held up a deprecating hand. "Don't fly off the handle, old bean. I didn't get in touch with you because I couldn't. You see I was inside that house when they set fire to it and couldn't very well—"

The news-editor gripped him by the shoulders, all his anger gone. He looked into the reporter's weary, humorous eyes and then swung away swiftly to the 'phone. "Tell Mackshott there's a big story coming," he ordered. "We'll run a special edition." He dashed down the receiver and turned again to Jimmie. "There won't be time for you to write it," he declared. "You must dictate. Half a moment."

His quick eye had appreciated that Silverdale was on the verge of utter exhaustion. He gave swift orders to a boy who, galvanized into activity, slipped over to the Paper Club for brandy and coffee. Thus stimulated, Jimmie began his big story—the biggest story, outside the war, of his career.

Every person in the building who could write shorthand was pressed into service, for minutes gained meant pounds saved in special trains. Watch in hand, the news-editor touched each man on the shoulder at the end of two minutes and the writer almost without pause would take up the work of transcription while another followed Silverdale's dictation. The chief sub snatched the slips as they were finished, numbered them consecutively and corrected slight errors and jammed them into pneumatic tubes to be shot up to the composing room.

Silverdale had often noticed that a state of acute physical exhaustion re-acted as a stimulant on his mind. He formulated his phrases and the sequence of his story clearly, and as he came the fight in the tunnel, he knew he was, in the words of Fleet Street, "getting there."

The news-editor's eyes glistened and he licked his lips appreciatively. Here was a big story told in a big way. Yet Jimmie had not unduly stressed those parts of the episode of which he did not wish the public to have too close an appreciation. Only where he himself was concerned did he let himself go large. That had to be done. He was a part of the paper. Jimmie Silverdale would have preferred to shine a little less conspicuously.

As the representative of the *Daily Wire*, he was forced to sink his modesty.

It was an hour before he finished. The news-editor slapped him lightly on the back. "This will make our obscure and loathsome contemporaries sit up, Jimmie," he said. "You're one of the seven wonders of the world."

"Yes," said Jimmie listlessly.

"What are you going to do now?"

"Go home and have a sleep. There'll be the wind-up of the yarn to do to-morrow and then I'm going to have a holiday."

"You've earned it," agreed the other.

"As a fact," said Jimmie in a burst of confidence, "I'm going to get married."

"The devil you are. I never thought you were a marrying man. Who's the poor deluded victim?"

Jimmie was rolling another cigarette with slow, nervous fingers. "It's the best girl in the world," he said. "She's a lady of the name of Hilary Sloane."

The news-editor whistled. "I begin to understand a lot of things that puzzled me," he said. "Well, good luck, Jimmie."

Silverdale slept like a log that night—a sleep of pure exhaustion. When he awoke, it was after ten o'clock and he could hear the newsboys in the streets. He smiled happily and bathed and dressed before he looked at the paper. Sprawled right across the main page was a big headline.

THE SIEGE OF CELLO STREET
*The Daily Wire Unmasks Great Murder
Conspiracy*
WHO KILLED HAROLD SAXON?
*Exclusive Story of Battle with Revolvers i/n
Underground Tunnel Beneath Burning
Gambling Hell.—Vivid Story of Daily Wire
Representative Who Was Imprisoned by
Prisoner.*

SEVERAL ARRESTS
(By JAMES SILVERDALE—Our Special
Correspondent)

Jimmie smiled happily. This was the sort of thing that made life worth living.

An hour later he found Garfield at Scotland Yard. The chief detective inspector admitted to two hours' sleep in an armchair and confessed to Jimmie that he felt a trifle wearied. Yes, he had had Miss Sloane escorted safely home and everything was looking promising.

"Just for to-day, we're going to charge Eston with attempting to murder you," he said.

"There'll only be formal evidence of arrest and we'll get a remand till we're good and ready to go on."

"How about Miss Dring?"

Garfield sucked at his pipe. "In hospital and not expected to live. She was shot through the lungs. She's conscious and I'm going to try to get a statement from her if the doctors permit."

"I'll go with you," said Jimmie.

All that day he acted as Garfield's shadow and the chief inspector was a very busy man. The organization of such a prosecution as it was intended to initiate was in itself no light business and Scotland Yard had to supply the Public Prosecutors' Department with all the material on which to act. It was after midday when they received an intimation that Nora Dring, though very weak, was in a condition when she might be questioned. Accompanied by a magistrate, they found the girl breathing painfully, her vivid hair forming a startling splash of color on the white cot where she rested, a doctor by her side. She turned a white pain-drawn face towards them. Silverdale, who had flashes of sentiment, laid a bunch of roses at the foot of the bed.

"Thank you," she gasped. "I scarcely deserve them, do I?"

"I am sorry to worry you like this," said Garfield. "We

should not have worried you but it is essential in the interests of justice that you answer a few questions. You will understand that you are not forced to answer. You may refuse if you like. You ought to know that your condition is serious."

"I'm dying," said the girl placidly. "I know it."

"Your condition is very grave," said the doctor. "But there is a chance—a remote chance."

"Don't trouble to deceive me," she said grimly. "I'm going to die. I'm terribly afraid that it's not so dreadful as I thought."

"I want to know what you know of the murder of Sir Harold Saxon," said Garfield quietly. "Did Eston have any concern in it?"

She raised herself on one elbow. "You know I was his wife," she said. "You know I killed him!" Her eyes, unnaturally bright, sought Garfield's questioningly.

"I know that," he said gravely. "Do you feel equal to telling us the whole story of your associations with him?"

XXVI

NORA DRING took a deep breath that was almost a sigh. Her long, graceful arm was lying on the coverlet, and she opened and shut her fist nervously.

"I wonder if there is a hell?" she said, slowly. "If so—" she stopped abruptly, and fell silent. "Well, I have deserved everything, I suppose. A girl who has acted as I have towards society, towards her best friend, can expect no other reward."

Jimmie Silverdale leaned forward impulsively.

"You—" he began.

The doctor shook his head warningly, and Garfield held up an admonitory forefinger.

"You have known Eston for a matter of months?" he asked.

"Longer than that. I knew him years ago, but he had been away from England, and we only resumed our acquaintanceship recently. I loved him. He is a soulless, implacable, relentless brute, yet I loved him! When I met him first, we were acquaintances. This time he sought me out, and I fell under his influence. He is a masterful man, and I loved him—"

"He did not know you were a married woman?" interposed the inspector quietly.

The girl stared at him with defiant, startled eyes.

"No. You know, then, that I am—that I am—"

"Lady Saxon. Yes, I know that. Don't exhaust yourself, please. There is nothing uncanny in my knowledge. It is my business to know. Let me give you some more details, and correct me if I am wrong. You went to America, some time back, in the hope of making more money than you could here? You called on several editors and publishers in an attempt to secure magazine and book illustrations?"

"That is true. I could not find a market here at that

time. I had to live by my own efforts."

"My information is that you did not find much of a market there," said Garfield dryly. "There is no magic in all this. I had your career traced out step by step by sheer hard work and pertinacious inquiry for the whole period during which you were over there. There is, however, one thing that puzzled me. Why should you have used the name of Hilary Sloane instead of your own?"

She thought for a moment.

"It was a mad freak," she admitted at last —"a mere mad, dishonest freak. I had some color sketches of Hilary's in my portfolio, and the first editor I called upon picked upon two of them for use as magazine covers. I had not the courage to own that the signature they bore was not mine. He had not caught my name, and addressed me as 'Miss Sloane.' I never realized that it could do any harm to Hilary."

"So you stuck to your friend's name all through the piece? Now I begin to understand something that had baffled me. Well, things didn't go so well as you anticipated? You found yourself very hard up, and you ultimately met Saxon and married him—still as Hilary Sloane?"

"Yes."

"You lived with him less than a month; then there was a violent quarrel, and you separated?"

She lifted a thin hand in dissent, and shook her head wearily.

"We did not separate. He threw me out. I was left, penniless and hopeless, in a strange land!" Her voice took on a new vehement note. "Is it any wonder that I swore the time should come when I would repay—repay in full, with interest pressed down and running over? I have done what I swore to do! So far as Harold Saxon is concerned, I have no regrets!"

"But Eston knew nothing of this?"

"No, he knew nothing—nothing, that is, of my marriage to Saxon. But he knew that I hated the man—

that I would go to any lengths to achieve a fitting punishment. He had asked me what I knew of Saxon on one occasion, and though I said little, I said enough. Thereafter, he played on my lust for vengeance."

"Ah!" Garfield glanced significantly at Silverdale and hurriedly added some notes to a pad he was holding in his hand. "He offered to help you to—organize a method by which you could achieve your ends—and yet escape justice?"

"I don't know how you know that, but that is exactly what happened. It all came suddenly at last. . I 'phoned him one day, and was warned to go to Saxon's flat in St. Ronan's Place at a certain time. I was to find the door open, and to walk right in. There was no one there when I entered—only Saxon—tied to a chair and unconscious. I used a hatpin—the only weapon I had—and killed him!"

Silverdale shuddered.

"I was in a kind of dream," went on the girl. "I was not in the place five minutes, and have no recollection what happened afterwards, till I found myself walking in Hyde Park. Then it all came back. I realized that I was a murderess—that the police would be upon my trail, and that, despite Eston's assurances, I might find myself in the dock. The hangman's noose haunted me. I lost my nerve. I went home. There I found Hilary. Without giving her any hint as to my reason, I insisted that I must leave London secretly. I was distraught with panic. She was the loyal friend she has always been. She asked questions, but when I refused to answer them, she accepted my refusal, and promised to do what she could to help me. You know what has happened since."

"Thank you," said Garfield. "I will not worry you any more now. In half an hour you will be shown a written statement embodying what you have told us. You will sign it?"

She studied him curiously for a moment.

"What of Mr. Eston?" she asked. "Will it hurt him? What has happened to him?"

"You will be told all that when you are better," said Garfield soothingly. "You will sign the statement?"

"No," she said resolutely, and sank back on the pillow. The doctor was bending over her.

"I think you had better leave her, gentlemen," he said. "She has drawn too much on her vitality. She has fainted."

"The ways of women are past finding out!" commented Garfield, as he and Silverdale left the room.

XXVII

IN the chief detective inspector's room at New Scotland Yard, Garfield perched himself on a high stool and fiddled with a thick batch of documents. Silverdale rolled himself a cigarette and found himself a chair.

"I think two of the men who have been disillusioned in this affair," said Garfield, "have been Velvet Fred and Knuckleduster. They banked blindly on Eston, who has a certain quality of leadership, and they were staggered when they found he had lost the game. Fred is an adroit and dangerous rogue to a point, but he is easily influenced in certain ways. He was scared stiff after we had had that talk with him at St. Ronan's Place—and yet he was back playing the game with Eston about as soon as he left us. Now it was clear that, after what he told us he would not go back to Eston willingly. The bigger man had him completely terrorized and he must have grabbed him almost as soon as we let him go.

"Velvet has more brains than Jim, but he is the weaker of the two men, so I tackled him first. He was quaking like a jelly when I entered his cell and I knew he would say anything I wanted. I was afraid he might be too much inclined to say what he thought I wanted rather than the truth. Prisoners who have got wound up are that way sometimes.

"'I don't want any lies from you,' I told him. 'You may be charged as an accessory to murder, or you may not. If you can answer my questions frankly, we'll decide what to do about you.'

"He was in a pitiable condition. 'I couldn't help it,' he whined. 'It was Eston.'

"'Yes,' I said. 'You went to Eston after you left us and gave the whole show away so far as you were able. He might never have guessed we associated him with the business if it hadn't been for that. "Why did you do it?'

"Then, at last, it began to come out. The poor devil was bound to Eston by two ties. In the first place he sincerely believed that Eston would do him in some way unless he made some amends for having told us something. In the second place, Eston was a good paymaster and had promised Velvet that if the big scheme he had in hand came off, Velvet Fred would be well in it to the extent of £50,000."

Jimmie Silverdale knocked the ash off his cigarette. "Did Velvet believe that?" he asked.

"Well, mutual trust has not, in my experience, always been a distinguishing characteristic of thieves. Still, from Velvet Fred's point, there was a possibility to make his mouth water. If he stood out, there was the certainty of Eston's vengeance. I don't think myself that Eston would have killed him. What I imagine would have happened would be that we —the police—would get an anonymous tip and Velvet would have somehow been found in very compromising circumstances. These things have occurred. Anyway, whatever the reason, Fred was for Eston. He was not on the inside —Eston was not showing his hand to any accomplice if he could help it. Velvet had to do what he was told and to make guesses.

"Nor was Knuckleduster Jim anything but an instrument. He is a different type from Velvet. He has less brains but is more of a tough. He is dogged as a bulldog and not at all averse from violence. I got him talking when I told him Eston had fallen into our trap, and he has since made a voluntary statement. I was able to convince him that I knew a great deal by using what Velvet had told me, or guessed at.

"Between the two of them, the story becomes more or less straightforward, added to what we already know. Eston had been planning his scheme for months. Whether Nora Dring was part of the original plot or not, one cannot be certain. Eston would naturally take measures to get into association with Hilary Sloane, and had probably schemed to do it through some mutual friend. When he discovered that Miss Dring was an old acquaintance, it simplified matters from his point of view. He was able the more completely to influence her.

"Now as I have said, Knuckleduster was not the sort of man to shrink from the part for which Eston had cast him. Mind you, I think he would, at that time, have hesitated at murder. On the other hand, Nora Dring could not be trusted to effectively dispose of an able-bodied man like Harold Saxon if he was at liberty to defend himself.

"So, first of all, Eston has the flat burgled by Velvet—for papers, mark you. Obviously he wanted a marriage certificate. Then he lured away the housekeeper with a bogus message and let Knuckleduster loose with instructions that he was to tie up Saxon and leave him. He gave Jim to understand at that time that it was a question of blackmail and that in case things went wrong, he wished to have Saxon helpless after an interview he proposed to have with the aeroplane manufacturer.

"As a matter of fact, of course he never intended to go near the flat. He got in touch with the Dring woman and the affair came off as he had planned. Once the murder was committed, neither Knuckleduster nor Velvet could fail to appreciate that Eston had been playing an even deeper game than they had realized. But by that time they were involved—particularly Jim. Eston explained to him that the murder was sheer coincidence, but Knuckleduster knew exactly how much value to put upon that.

"I don't suppose Knuckleduster had any qualms of conscience but he recognized that, if ever the worst came to the worst, his story of innocent complicity in the murder was liable to be disbelieved. He was not altogether reluctant to throw his hand in with Eston.

"That, Jimmie, is in effect, where we stand at this moment with the case. There are a few minor people round the edges who helped Eston in various ways, but they will not matter to any great extent."

The telephone bell jangled and Garfield slid off the high stool to answer it. "Hello! . . . Hello! . . .Yes, this is Garfield. . . .Yes! . . . Ah, thank you." He put down the receiver and turned towards Silverdale.

"Miss Nora Dring died in hospital half an hour ago."

Jimmie nodded solemnly. "I'll not say I'm sorry. For her it is perhaps the best thing that could have happened."

"It is the end of an episode," agreed Garfield.

XXVIII

MEN do curious, things after they have passed through great stress. Eston with the possibility of a fate that might well have kept him wakeful, shrugged his shoulders after the formalities of his arrival at the police-station had been complied with, flung himself at full length on the hard couch in his cell and in a matter of seconds was asleep. For twelve hours he lay and was only roused at last by the abrupt grip of the jailer on his shoulder.

"Don't you want anything to eat? It's gone two."

Eston sat up, yawned, and stretched himself while he collected his thoughts. It was difficult off-hand for him to realize that he had reached the end. He frowned thoughtfully at the police-officer who had charge of the station-cells.

"Don't you want some grub sent in?" asked that functionary.

A man under detention at a police-station is entitled if he cares to do so to have his meals purchased and sent in from outside. The police authorities as caterers are a little circumscribed. Eston understood the procedure.

"I'd like some coffee and bacon and eggs, if you can get them," he said. "Tell me, where am I to know what they are going to charge me with?"

"I can't tell you anything about that. I expect Mr. Garfield or someone will turn up during the day. Of course, if you want to see him—"

He paused expectantly, but Eston shook his head. "Right-oh! I'll see about your food."

As a fact, it was nearly seven o'clock that evening before any person other than the jailer intruded on

Eston's privacy. Then he was ushered upstairs to a room of the station allotted to a divisional branch of the Criminal Investigation Department. Silverdale and Garfield were there with one or two other men he did not recognize. Uniformed constables were holding him by each arm, yet Eston contrived to assume somehow a manner of nonchalant ease. This, he knew, was probably one of the opening stages in his fight for life, and he was wary, cool, and well on his guard. He even, arranged a smile.

"Let him go!" ordered Garfield quietly; and the policemen fell back. "Take a seat, Mr. Eston, won't you?"

"Thanks," said the prisoner.

He sat down, facing the inspector, and crossed his legs. It would have needed a very keen observer to detect any tone of anxiety in his voice or manner. Yet Eston was worried, and his heart beat faster than its wont as he sat there waiting for what might happen.

"You made a statement to me last night, or rather, early this morning," said the chief inspector. "I am going to read that over to you to give you an opportunity of rectifying or amending it."

Eston moistened dry lips.

"You read it to me then," he said. "Why go over it again?"

The chief inspector gave a significant jerk of the head.

"I want to be fair to you, Eston," he said.

The prisoner gave an ironical laugh.

Ignoring the interruption, Garfield went on:

"There are inconsistencies and contradictions in your statement with the facts as we know them. Now's your chance to remedy any point on which you went wrong."

He began reading. Eston listened attentively, a sardonic smile on his lips. Even then he was convinced that this was some new game of bluff set to entrap him into some damaging admission. Clever and unscrupulous man as he was, he was unable to conceive that he was being offered a real chance to amend his statement out of a sheer quixotic sense of fairness.

Smoothly, monotonously, Garfield read on. There were facts with which Eston could take no liberties, but on the other hand he had avoided any damaging admission of matters which it was possible the police would be unable to prove. He denied point-blank that he knew Sir Harold Saxon, or that he had had any guilty knowledge of the murder. The meeting with Hilary Sloane and Nora Dring at Twyford Station he pictured as a perfectly accidental happening, in which they had appealed to him as an old friend to help them in some trouble. He did not then fully understand what the trouble was. Thereafter the incidents that occurred were the fruits of an altruistic chivalry that had led to compromising situations. The fire in the gambling house was sheer accident.

He made no attempt to deny the fight in the tunnel. Indeed, the bulk of the statement, clever and plausible though it was, was intended as the background upon which an ultimate defense might be founded by a clever lawyer. Eston was cutting his losses. It was on the river question that he had concentrated his,resources. He had a complete and unquestionable alibi provable by a dozen witnesses as to Sir Harold Saxon's murder. On that he had taken infinite pains. If he went to prison—well, some day he would come out. If he were convicted of murder!

"That's your statement," finished Garfield quietly. "Now I know as well as you do, Eston, that it's a tissue of lies!"

Eston flared at him defiantly.

"If you've made up your mind about it, why trouble me?" he asked.

"Every inquiry we have made," went on Garfield, "fails to substantiate anything you say, except that it is clear that you were not present at the actual murder of Sir Harold Saxon. It is only right you should know that Knuckleduster and Velvet have told their stories."

"Really?" Eston's voice was icy. "I don't quite see how

that can concern me. I have told the truth."

"You have nothing further to add—nothing to explain?"

The crook shook his head doggedly.

"I have been quite frank."

"Then we'll finish this farce," said Garfield sternly.

Eston, a constable at each elbow, found himself heading a procession down the narrow stairs into a lofty, bare charge-room. In the center of the room stood a solitary tall desk, against which leaned a meditative uniformed inspector, a pen behind his ear. He straightened up briskly as the little group entered, and became busy with an official form.

Eston was led near the little iron dock that forms part of the fittings of every London charge-room, and is never used, and waited. Garfield strolled over to the uniformed inspector, and spoke in a low voice, while the other wrote rapidly. Eston regarded them with an apparent listless indifference that marked a very real alertness of mind. Little legal phrases, repeated by one or the other, caught his ear now and again.

"Henry John Eston?" said the uniformed man at last.

Eston muttered an assent.

"You are charged at the instance of Chief- Detective Inspector Garfield that you did kill and murder Sir Harold Saxon—"

"What!"

After his careful alibi, Eston was staggered. It was incredible, impossible, that the murder could really be brought home to him.

"That is utterly false. I had nothing to do with that, as Mr. Garfield knows very well."

Garfield held up a warning hand.

"In law, a person who plans and incites a murder is as guilty as a person who actually commits the deed," he said. "You know that, although Knuckleduster Jim and Nora Dring were your dupes, Harold Saxon might have been alive at this moment had it not been for you."

A constable put out a hand to steady the prisoner, who reeled slightly on his feet. A curious flush spread over his face that was succeeded by a sickly pallor. He spread out his hands helplessly.

"Have they talked?" he demanded.

Garfield nodded grimly.

Then Eston got some sort of a grip on his reeling senses. It was impossible that all his precautions could go for nothing. It is only an innocent man who is utterly confounded by an unexpected charge. What, he reflected, could they prove, after all? If Knuckleduster had squealed—he still clung to the "if"—there would still be considerable difficulty in linking up his connection with the capital charge. Garfield was bluffing. He was sure of that.

"You are also charged," went on the monotonous voice of the inspector, "that you did kill and murder Nora Saxon."

"Is she dead?" asked Eston.

"She died in hospital a little more than an hour ago," said Garfield.

In a daze, Eston heard the recital, in its quaint, legal jargon, go on.

"Did feloniously attempt to kill and murder one James Silverdale. Did commit arson."

It ended at last.

"Those are the charges against you, Eston," concluded the man at the desk. "If you have any reply to make, it will be taken down in writing, and may be used as evidence against you."

A sudden access of inner rage shook the prisoner. His fists clenched and his whole form quivered.

"It's a lie!" he declared vehemently. "A series of dastardly, abominable lies! Curse you, Garfield!"

"That will be all," said the station-inspector, without emotion. "Take him below."

Unresisting, Eston allowed himself to be escorted back to his cell.

XXIX

IN no phase of life is the shortness of the public memory more evident than, in the newspaper profession. Within six months the names of many of those who figured in the blaze of publicity that made the Saxon murder case a theme of vivid interest to the man in the street had faded almost out of memory. There were other and more immediate things to occupy the public mind. And yet for three long months the case had dragged over the coroner's court, the police-court, to the Central Criminal Court at the Old Bailey. Eston himself was always certain of a niche of infamy in the minds of a certain section of the public; but, then, Eston was hanged. Beyond that, the details of the case were obscured to most people.

It may be that this shortness of public memory is a deliberate device on the part of Providence for the benefit of those innocent people who must be concerned in every great case. Neither Garfield nor his colleagues had any objection to publicity once the matter had reached the court.

Jimmie Silverdale, however, came to hate the sight of his name in a descriptive report, though he fully appreciated the irony of a journalist figuring in a *cause celebre*. He was even more concerned, however, by the prominence afforded to Hilary.

To lawyers, to court officials, to news-editors, and to his fellow-reporters, he appeared at various times to stagemanage Hilary's part of the affairs as quietly as possible. Mostly, they would have gone far to oblige Jimmie, but the momentum of the facts was too much for them. Hilary was well in the picture, and Silverdale ground his teeth with impotence. It was one thing to start a big story, and quite another to stop it.

On that sultry July evening when the jury had retired for the last time, Jimmie escorted Hilary out of court, and returned to his seat beneath the jurybox. Eston, pale, with tight-pressed lips, glanced in that direction as he was escorted back to the dock to hear his fate.

His eyes met Jimmie's full, and, for the fraction of a second he smiled—a harassed, ghastly smile, but still a smile. Almost instantly his face had became again impassive, and his gaze sought the foreman who, a small piece of paper gripped tightly in his hand, stood standing facing the Clerk of Arraigns.

"Gentlemen of the jury, do you find the prisoner guilty or not guilty?"

Silverdale had witnessed many such scenes, but this somehow had him by the throat. He slipped away to join Hilary, the solemn, deep-throated warning of the usher preceding the sentence of death coming faintly to him:

"Oyez! Oyez! Oyez!"

After that, it was a matter of small moment that Knuckleduster Jim had been sentenced to fifteen years' penal servitude, and Velvet Fred to five. The thing was over. Some of the papers had short homilies in their leader columns next day which were not read, and many columns descriptive of the closing scenes of the trial, which were widely read. Thereafter the big story was over. It had burnt out.

.   .   .   .   .

There remains only one more episode. At a little church in an unfashionable locality, some three months later, the news-editor of the *Daily Wire*, resplendent in morning-coat and silk hat, waited on the steps with quiet amusement, while the hatchet-faced young man with him fidgeted with his watch.

"I hope nothing has happened," said Jimmie Silverdale impatiently.

His friend grinned unfeelingly.

"The lady's due in, perhaps, ten minutes, my lad. Keep calm, like a good newspaperman. You're behaving lite a bridegroom out of the comic papers!"

"I feel like one," agreed Jimmie. "You're sure you have got that ring all right?"

"Sure. . . . Here they come!"

A motor slid to a standstill. Chief-Detective Inspector Garfield, huge and smiling, offered his hand to the bride, and the news-editor hustled Jimmie into the church, lest the etiquette of these affairs should be violated. So the ceremony proceeded. Not until they were at breakfast in the hotel, where a quiet reception had been arranged, did the news-editor speak his mind.

"Jimmie Silverdale," he said, in a speech he had prepared for the toast of the bride and groom, "has been the best newspaperman I have known in a long experience. Let me warn you, Mrs. Silverdale, that one of two things must happen. If he continues to be a good newspaperman, he will be a bad husband, and if he becomes a good husband, he will be a bad newspaperman."

Hilary clung to her husband's arm.

"I'll take the risk," she said.

THE END

Resurrected Press Books in A. E. Fielding's *The Chief Inspector Pointer Mystery* Series

The Eames-Erskine Case (1924)
The Charteris Mystery (1925)
The Footsteps that Stopped (1926)
The Clifford Affair (1927)
The Cluny Problem (1928)
The Net Around Joan Ingilby (1928)
The Murder at the Nook (1929)
The Mysterious Partner (1929)
The Craig Poisoning Mystery (1930)
The Wedding Chest Mystery (1930)
The Upfold Farm Mystery (1931)
Death of John Tait (1932)
The Westwood Mystery (1932)
The Tall House Mystery (1933)
The Cautley Conundrum (1934)
The Paper-Chase (1934)
The Case of the Missing Diary (1935)
Tragedy at Beechcroft (1935)
The Case of the Two Pearl Necklaces (1935)
Mystery at the Rectory (1936)
Black Cats Are Lucky (1937)
Scarecrow (1937)
Pointer to a Crime (1944)

MORE MYSTERIES BY LEONARD GRIBBLE

**Available now, or coming Soon!
Like us on Facebook to see our latest books!
http://www.facebook.com/ResurrectedPress**

AVAILABLE FROM RESURRECTED PRESS!

THE EDWARDIAN DETECTIVES
LITERARY SLEUTHS OF THE EDWARDIAN ERA

The exploits of the great Victorian Detectives, Poe's C. Auguste Dupin, Gaboriau's Lecoq, and most famously, Arthur Conan Doyle's Sherlock Holmes, are well known. But what of those fictional detectives that came after, those of the Edwardian Age? The period between the death of Queen Victoria and the First World War had been called the Golden Age of the detective short story, but how familiar is the modern reader with the sleuths of this era? And such an extraordinary group they were, including in their numbers an unassuming English priest, a blind man, a master of disguises, a lecturer in medical jurisprudence, a noble woman working for Scotland Yard, and a savant so brilliant he was known as "The Thinking Machine."

To introduce readers to these detectives, Resurrected Press has assembled a collection of stories featuring these and other remarkable sleuths in The Edwardian Detectives.

- The Case of Laker, Absconded by Arthur Morrison
- The Fenchurch Street Mystery by Baroness Orczy
- The Crime of the French Café by Nick Carter
- The Man with Nailed Shoes by R Austin Freeman
- The Blue Cross by G. K. Chesterton
- The Case of the Pocket Diary Found in the Snow by Augusta Groner
- The Ninescore Mystery by Baroness Orczy
- The Riddle of the Ninth Finger by Thomas W. Hanshew
- The Knight's Cross Signal Problem by Ernest Bramah

- The Problem of Cell 13 by Jacques Futrelle
- The Conundrum of the Golf Links by Percy James Brebner
- The Silkworms of Florence by Clifford Ashdown
- The Gateway of the Monster by William Hope Hodgson
- The Affair at the Semiramis Hotel by A. E. W. Mason
- The Affair of the Avalanche Bicycle & Tyre Co., LTD by Arthur Morrison

RESURRECTED PRESS CLASSIC
MYSTERY CATALOGUE

Journeys into Mystery
Travel and Mystery in a More Elegant Time

The Edwardian Detectives
Literary Sleuths of the Edwardian Era

Gems of Mystery
Lost Jewels from a More Elegant Age

E. C. Bentley
Trent's Last Case: The Woman in Black

Ernest Bramah
Max Carrados Resurrected:
The Detective Stories of Max Carrados

Agatha Christie
The Secret Adversary
The Mysterious Affair at Styles

Octavus Roy Cohen
Midnight

Freeman Wills Croft
The Ponson Case
The Pit Prop Syndicate

J. S. Fletcher
The Herapath Property
The Rayner-Slade Amalgamation
The Chestermarke Instinct
The Paradise Mystery
Dead Men's Money

The Middle of Things
Ravensdene Court
Scarhaven Keep
The Orange-Yellow Diamond
The Middle Temple Murder
The Tallyrand Maxim
The Borough Treasurer
In the Mayor's Parlour
The Saftey Pin

R. Austin Freeman
*The Mystery of 31 New Inn from the Dr. Thorndyke
Series*
*John Thorndyke's Cases from the Dr. Thorndyke
Series*
The Red Thumb Mark from The Dr. Thorndyke Series
The Eye of Osiris from The Dr. Thorndyke Series
A Silent Witness from the Dr. John Thorndyke Series
The Cat's Eye from the Dr. John Thorndyke Series
*Helen Vardon's Confession: A Dr. John Thorndyke
Story*
As a Thief in the Night: A Dr. John Thorndyke Story
*Mr. Pottermack's Oversight: A Dr. John Thorndyke
Story*
*Dr. Thorndyke Intervenes: A Dr. John Thorndyke
Story*
The Singing Bone: The Adventures of Dr. Thorndyke
The Stoneware Monkey: A Dr. John Thorndyke Story
*The Great Portrait Mystery, and Other Stories: A
Collection of Dr. John Thorndyke and Other Stories*
The Penrose Mystery: A Dr. John Thorndyke Story
The Uttermost Farthing: A Savant's Vendetta

Arthur Griffiths
The Passenger From Calais
The Rome Express

Louis Tracy
The Strange Case of Mortimer Fenley
The Albert Gate Mystery
The Bartlett Mystery
The Postmaster's Daughter
The House of Peril
The Sandling Case: What Would You Have Done?
Charles Edmonds Walk
The Paternoster Ruby

John R. Watson
The Mystery of the Downs
The Hampstead Mystery

Edgar Wallace
The Daffodil Mystery
The Crimson Circle

Carolyn Wells
Vicky Van
The Man Who Fell Through the Earth
In the Onyx Lobby
Raspberry Jam
The Clue
The Room with the Tassels
The Vanishing of Betty Varian
The Mystery Girl
The White Alley
The Curved Blades
Anybody but Anne
The Bride of a Moment
Faulkner's Folly
The Diamond Pin
The Gold Bag
The Mystery of the Sycamore
The Come Backy

Raoul Whitfield
Death in a Bowl

And much more!
Visit ResurrectedPress.com
for our complete catalogue

About Resurrected Press

A division of Intrepid Ink, LLC, Resurrected Press is dedicated to bringing high quality, vintage books back into publication. See our entire catalogue and find out more at www.ResurrectedPress.com.

About Intrepid Ink, LLC

Intrepid Ink, LLC provides full publishing services to authors of fiction and non-fiction books, eBooks and websites. From editing to formatting, from publishing to marketing, Intrepid Ink gets your creative works into the hands of the people who want to read them. Find out more at www.IntrepidInk.com.